"I'm pregna___

Logan didn't sa___ ___uld see his jaw tense, and finally, as hours seemed to pass, she heard him blow out a breath. Still, he remained silent.

"Go ahead, Logan," Meg said. "Tell me how you feel as if you're in the middle of history repeating itself."

"How do *you* feel?" he asked without responding to her statement.

Had she expected Logan to suddenly declare his undying love? Maybe she hadn't expected it, but searching her heart, she had to admit that had been a hope. "I'm confused and scared," she finally confessed.

"You don't have to go through it alone." There was sincerity in his voice, but distance, too.

And any hope Meg had entertained about happily-ever-after slowly wilted away.

Dear Reader,

It's that joyful time of year again! And Santa has some wonderfully festive books coming your way this December.

Bestselling author Marie Ferrarella brings you our THAT'S MY BABY! for December. This holiday bundle of joy is still a secret to his or her dad...and Mom is sure to be a *Christmas Bride*.

And the patter of little feet doesn't stop there. Don't miss *A Baby for Rebecca* by Trisha Alexander, the latest in her THREE BRIDES AND A BABY miniseries. *Holly and Mistletoe* is Susan Mallery's newest title in the HOMETOWN HEARTBREAKERS miniseries, a tale filled with Christmas warmth and love. And for those of you who've been enjoying Tracy Sinclair's CUPID'S LITTLE HELPERS miniseries, this month we've got *Mandy Meets a Millionaire*—with the help of some little matchmakers.

December also brings Diana Whitney's *Barefoot Bride*—the heroine is an amnesiac woman in a wedding dress who finds love with a single dad and his kids at Christmastime. This is the second book in Diana's wonderful PARENTHOOD miniseries. *The Sheriff's Proposal* by Karen Rose Smith is a warm, tender tale that takes place during the season of giving.

I hope you enjoy all our books this month. All of us here at Silhouette wish you a happy, healthy holiday season!

Sincerely,

Tara Gavin
Senior Editor

Please address questions and book requests to:
Silhouette Reader Service
U.S.: 3010 Walden Ave., P.O. Box 1325, Buffalo, NY 14269
Canadian: P.O. Box 609, Fort Erie, Ont. L2A 5X3

KAREN ROSE SMITH

THE SHERIFF'S PROPOSAL

SPECIAL EDITION®

Published by Silhouette Books
America's Publisher of Contemporary Romance

To my husband, Steve. Happy twenty-fifth
anniversary. I love you.

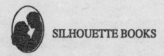 SILHOUETTE BOOKS

ISBN 0-373-24074-0

THE SHERIFF'S PROPOSAL

Copyright © 1996 by Karen Rose Smith

All rights reserved. Except for use in any review, the reproduction or utilization of this work in whole or in part in any form by any electronic, mechanical or other means, now known or hereafter invented, including xerography, photocopying and recording, or in any information storage or retrieval system, is forbidden without the written permission of the editorial office, Silhouette Books, 300 East 42nd Street, New York, NY 10017 U.S.A.

All characters in this book have no existence outside the imagination of the author and have no relation whatsoever to anyone bearing the same name or names. They are not even distantly inspired by any individual known or unknown to the author, and all incidents are pure invention.

This edition published by arrangement with Harlequin Books S.A.

® and TM are trademarks of Harlequin Books S.A., used under license. Trademarks indicated with ® are registered in the United States Patent and Trademark Office, the Canadian Trade Marks Office and in other countries.

Printed in U.S.A.

KAREN ROSE SMITH

admits her characters are as real to her as her friends. While writing a romance, she becomes involved in her characters' lives, their emotions and their conflicts. She especially loves writing the last few chapters, finally bringing her hero and heroine together so they can find their happily-ever-after.

A wife, mother and former educator, Karen is now a full-time writer. She lives in Hanover, Pennsylvania, with her husband. She enjoys hearing from readers. They can write to her at P.O. Box 1545, Hanover, PA 17331.

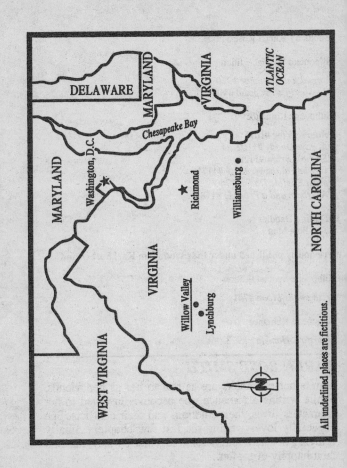

All underlined places are fictitious.

Chapter One

Sheriff Logan MacDonald's office phone rang making his heart ache and pound at the same time. At the Willow Valley sheriff's office, a phone call could mean a life-and-death situation or, more likely, a few cows had escaped their fencing and blocked a county road. A call could also bring Logan news of his son.

But now after four months, when he answered a call or page, he tried to keep his heart from racing and his hopes from rising. Still, an insistent voice inside him whispered, *This could be the one. Maybe it's news of Travis.*

He snatched up the receiver.

"Doc Jacobs, Logan. I'm on my way over to Lily and Ned Carlson's. They found a migrant couple in their barn. The woman's having a baby, and they don't want the rescue squad. But I might need some backup."

Logan's heart rate slowed, and his hopes hit the ground. Then Doc Jacobs's words sunk in. The rescue squad in Willow Valley, Virginia, took care of the small town and the surrounding rural area. The closest hospital was a half hour away in Lynchburg. "I'm leaving now."

Logan snapped down the receiver and tried to push thoughts of his sixteen-year-old runaway son out of his head.

Although it was midmorning, the steamy, end-of-August heat blasted him as he hurried to his car. The temperature would probably hit a hundred by three o'clock. He could have sent one of his six deputies to the Carlsons' place, but he preferred taking some time out from his administrative duties and getting into the thick of things himself.

The inside of the sheriff's cruiser was as hot as blazes. He flipped on the air conditioner full blast, letting the panel air hit him in the face. He tried to forget that his hopes had been crushed yet another time, that he still didn't know whether his son was alive or dead. Four months. Four long months to agonize over every mistake he'd made as a parent.

Logan brushed his black hair from his brow as the cool air fought the intense heat, and he switched on the siren. The stores on Main Street flashed by, then the corner grocery. A few teenagers stood out front, reminding Logan that school would be starting in a week. And Travis . . .

Travis. Logan's chest tightened.

He had moved his family to Willow Valley five years ago in large part *because* of Travis. Logan had wanted more time with his son in a wholesome country environment, rather than on the streets of a big city. His career as a cop had always added tension to a marriage that had been troubled from the start. Even Shelley had agreed that moving might help—that a job as deputy sheriff in Willow Valley and the surrounding county could make a difference in their lives. But their son had hated leaving the familiar—his school, his friends.

And Shelley? She'd never had any intention of starting over. Once they were settled in Willow Valley, Logan had figured they'd all have a chance at a fresh start. But he'd figured wrong. For his marriage. For Travis.

The farmland surrounding Willow Valley zipped by as Logan sped toward the Carlsons' farm west of town. The green pastures, the cedars, the trees in abundance, usually filled him with a sense of peace. Even now he felt it, although his surroundings blurred as he pushed down the accelerator.

Logan drove down the lane to the Carlsons' barn and parked on a patch of gravel beside Doc Jacobs's station wagon. He didn't recognize the blue compact beside it, though he guessed it might belong to the Carlsons' niece. He'd never met her, but he'd heard she was in town for a visit. As small towns go, anything happening in Willow Valley was everybody's business, and rumors, as well as accurate information, traveled faster than the rescue squad with its siren blaring.

He rushed to the open barn door and stepped inside. The smell of hay and old wood wound about Logan. But when he heard a woman's moans, he forgot about his surroundings and hurried to the far corner. Although he'd learned CPR and emergency-aid training as a police officer, he'd never delivered a baby. He'd been out on patrol when Travis was born. But if Doc needed help, he'd do whatever he could.

The tableau Logan found was one he wouldn't forget for a long time. The woman in labor held on to her husband's hand. A second woman kneeling beside her spoke to them both in a low voice. Her fluent Spanish was melodic and soothing, a calm in the midst of a strange situation. She looked vaguely familiar. The observer and investigator in Logan noticed every detail—from the slight tilt of her nose, the silkiness of the brown hair swinging along her cheekbones, to her eyes, which were a rich chocolate color that deepened as she suddenly realized someone else was in their midst. Her gaze slid over his uniform. Logan's body responded to her figure in denim cutoffs and blue-and-white-checked cotton blouse. He almost smiled. That hadn't happened in a very long time.

Again she spoke to the woman lying on a blanket, patted her hand and explained something in Spanish. But it wasn't her talent with the language that mesmerized Logan. It was her tone of voice, her smile. She was so kind, so compassionate. Then her gaze rested on Logan's again for a moment. As it did, the place inside of him that hurt so badly suddenly felt a glimmer of sunshine.

"How can I help?" he asked, his voice husky. He cleared his throat.

Doc Jacobs looked up from his position at the woman's feet. "We're letting nature take its course. Hold her shoulders for her, Meg, or tell Manuel. This last push ought to do it. Come on now, Carmen. Give it all you've got."

As Carmen moaned and another contraction gripped her, the young woman beside her translated what the doctor had said. Logan had a limited working knowledge of Spanish, and he could catch a phrase here and there as Manuel held his wife, and Meg coached and soothed.

Logan forgot his purpose, that he was the law-and-order keeper in Willow Valley. Rather, he got caught up in the drama before him. It brought back so many memories, both good and bad. He'd never forget the day Travis was born, the sense of pride, the overwhelming wave of protectiveness and responsibility that had washed over him the first time he'd held his son in his arms. He'd never regretted his decision to marry Shelley when he'd found out she was pregnant. He did regret the interests they'd never shared, the conversations they'd never had, the barrier that had grown between them until Shelley had felt deception was her only option. Most of all, he regretted the night of their worst argument—the night she'd rushed out of the house and . . .

Carmen's face contorted in pain, and she squeezed Meg's hand. Her husband spoke to her, and Logan heard, *"Te quiero tanto."* "I love you very much." His throat constricted.

Logan absorbed all of it—the love between the couple, the soft, caring voice of the woman acting as interpreter and coach, the tears in her eyes as they all heard the first cry. And then it was over, yet in most ways it had just begun.

The doctor suctioned the baby's mouth, wrapped him in a towel and laid him on his mother's stomach. Manuel kissed Carmen, and they gazed at their child.

Doc said, "Meg, why don't you get some fresh air?"

"I'm okay, Doc."

"Yes, I know you are, but I'm not going to need you again until after I clean up the baby," replied Doc Jacobs, who tended to act as if he were everyone's father. "I'll call you if Carmen and Manuel want you. Now, scoot. Go get Lily. I know she'll want to help, too."

Logan waited for the woman who could speak Spanish as fluently as she spoke English and walked with her to the door. Close to her in the hay-baked heat of the barn, he smelled the faint scent of roses. Perfume? Shampoo? Whatever it was, along with her lovely smile and gentle voice, it packed a wallop.

He let her precede him outside. His shirt stuck to his back, but except for the swath of pink on her cheeks, she didn't look as if she'd just helped deliver a baby.

He extended his hand to a lady whose smile could make him believe the sun would come up tomorrow. "I'm Logan MacDonald."

Meg had heard a little about the sheriff over the past few years from her aunt and uncle. Not much, just that he was a widower and he ran his jurisdiction with an iron hand. Yet he was well liked by the constituents who'd gotten to know him as a deputy and had elected him sheriff because of his reputation and career in law enforcement. She'd been aware of his presence as soon as he'd walked into the barn. Her experiences had led her to be acutely aware of her surroundings, the tiniest inflections and mannerisms. All were elements of communication.

What Logan MacDonald had come upon in the barn had affected him deeply. She could tell from his expression, the huskiness in his voice.

The birth had affected her, too. Though early, this baby had been no accident. Manuel and Carmen didn't have much, but they already had a nurturing love for this child, the kind of love Meg had only felt from Aunt Lily and Uncle Ned.

As Meg placed her hand in Logan MacDonald's, she was aware that his physique in his uniform spoke of authority; the open top two buttons of his dark brown shirt told her he was impatient with the heat. He was sleek and muscled—tall with black hair and green eyes that seemed to be searching hers for something. He looked almost fierce in his concentration.

"Meg Dawson," she returned as he gripped her hand. The touch of his skin against hers made her that much more conscious of the intensity in his green eyes. She felt warm and more than a little bothered.

Releasing her hand, he snapped his fingers. "That's it. Now I recognize you. Margaret Elizabeth Dawson—the interpreter. Your picture was on the front page of most newspapers in the country not so long ago. I didn't realize you were Lily and Ned's niece."

She'd shied away from the *Willow Valley Courier* and their attempts to persuade her to do an interview after the initial wire-service story ran. She'd wanted to recover and forget.

But Logan remembered the details. "You were taken hostage in Costa Rica with a diplomat and wounded when your kidnapper started shooting. Finally you talked him into letting you and Pomada go in exchange for a plane. He didn't even get off the runway before the officials nabbed him. You should have been given a medal!"

She could feel her face turning pink. She hadn't even blushed when the president of the United States himself had shaken her hand. Of course, she might have still been in shock then. Part of her still was. "We got out alive. I didn't care about a medal," she said softly.

Her heart rate increased as Logan studied her. Standing in the shade of the barn, she noticed the strands of silver along his temples, the slight beard shadow that she guessed would grow darker as the day progressed, the male scent of him that tightened her stomach in an exciting way. She willed her pulse to slow. She didn't feel strong enough yet to get involved with anyone, let alone with a man like Logan, who exuded authority, intensity and a quality that told her he was hurting right now for some reason. She'd seen it on his face before Carmen's baby had arrived. She could see it now as she looked into his eyes.

"Did you come to Willow Valley to hibernate?" he asked with a perception that rattled her.

There were so many reasons she'd come back. But she simply answered, "I feel safe here."

Before Logan could respond, Doc Jacobs emerged from the barn. "Meg, ask Lily and Ned if they can put Manuel and Carmen up for a few days."

Meg looked concerned. "Do you think Manuel will agree?"

"For Carmen's sake, I hope so. We'll work on him. Logan, any word on Travis?"

The same pain Meg had glimpsed on Logan's face earlier shadowed his features again. "No."

"Your P.I. have any new leads?"

"No. Nothing. But I have to believe he's still out there somewhere."

Doc Jacobs grasped Logan's arm. "I know you do. And this whole town's praying." He ducked back into the barn.

Meg knew she had to talk to her aunt and uncle, yet her focus was still on Logan and the tortured look on his face. But she didn't feel she could ask any questions.

The next moment, Logan seemed to compose himself, only the creases on his forehead hinting something more important was on his mind. "So, tell me what happened here today."

Suddenly fatigue settled over Meg, fatigue that told her she was healing but wasn't yet healed. She leaned against the rough wood of the barn. "Manuel and Carmen are migrants. Legal ones. They were on their way to Pennsylvania for the apple harvest. Manuel's brother is already there."

"I can guess the rest. They didn't expect Carmen to deliver until they arrived in Pennsylvania."

Meg nodded. "When Carmen's labor pain became intense last night, Manuel knew he had to stop. He thought he could deliver the baby himself, but he got scared and, when we found them in the barn, he let us call Doc."

"Why wouldn't Manuel and Carmen stay here a few days?" Logan asked, studying her carefully.

"Because Manuel is proud and won't take handouts. He insists he'll pay Doc."

"Doc'll cut his fee in half."

"Probably. But although Manuel doesn't speak English fluently, he does understand it fairly well and knows the score. Convincing him to stay could be a problem. These two are stubborn. Manuel parked his truck on Black Rock Road last night, and he carried Carmen across the fields to the barn so no one would hear them."

Logan looked away, to the willow tree not far from the house with its graceful branches silent and still in the August heat. After a pause, he said, "Manuel has to do what's best for his wife and child."

Something in Logan's voice told her he'd had to make that decision. "I hope he will. He loves Carmen very much. I can feel the bond between the two of them. It's the same kind my aunt and uncle have."

Logan faced her again. "How long are *you* going to stay in Willow Valley?"

She was more comfortable talking about Manuel than herself. "I'm not sure. I've already been here a month. But it's really hit me this time that my aunt and uncle are getting older. I think I'd like to stay until Thanksgiving, anyway." The explanation was reasonable, but she knew her decision to stay was more complicated than that.

Disconcerted by the sheriff's probing green eyes, Meg pushed away from the barn. "I'd better talk to Aunt Lily. It was nice meeting you, Sheriff MacDonald." She started toward the backyard.

"Meg?" His deep voice vibrated through her.

She turned. "Yes?"

"My name's Logan."

With the hint of a smile, she nodded and headed toward the house.

Logan watched Margaret Elizabeth Dawson disappear. But he still felt the impact of her searching brown eyes. He could have gone back to the office, but he told himself he had to make sure the situation here was under control. In Willow Valley, helping sometimes became more important than enforcing. He liked that.

A half hour later, he and Doc Jacobs carried an old door from the basement of the farmhouse to the barn.

Meg sat on the floor next to Carmen and Manuel, speaking in Spanish. Manuel looked agitated. All three stopped talking when he and Doc came closer.

Huffing and puffing, Doc helped Logan lower the door down to the straw-covered floor beside Carmen and her baby. "I'm getting too old for this," he grumbled.

"More like you should take the advice you give to your patients," Logan suggested blandly.

"I suppose you mean about trimming down and getting exercise. You're only forty, Logan. When you hit sixty, then you come tell me how easy it is to do that."

Logan caught Meg looking at him as if wondering what kind of physique was hidden under his clothes. Her appraisal sent a surge of desire through him. This time he almost welcomed it. He couldn't help but say to her in a low aside, "I jog."

Her cheeks pinkened. She avoided Logan's gaze and looked at Doc. "Lily says Manuel and his family are welcome to stay until Carmen feels well enough to travel, but Manuel won't agree."

"We go north," Manuel said in explanation.

Doc glared at the young Hispanic and said slowly, "Lily and Ned are good people. If they invited you to stay, they want you here. You must think of your wife and child."

Meg put her hand on Manuel's arm. "Carmen and the baby need a few days to get stronger. Do this for them."

His almost black eyes searched Meg's face, then his wife's. In halting English, he said, "We stay tonight." Then he lapsed into Spanish. *"Sólo esta noche."*

Doc nodded. "We'll start with that. Tomorrow's another day." He pointed to the door. "Manuel, you and Logan can carry Carmen to the house using that as a stretcher."

Meg asked Manuel, *"Lo entendió?"*

"Sí."

As Manuel helped Carmen and the baby get situated on the door, Meg slipped a folded towel under the mother's head. When she did, the edge of her sleeve caught on the corner of the door, pulling it above her shoulder. Logan saw nasty red lines, healing but not completely healed. He remembered she'd been shot in the shoulder. He wondered just how serious the injury had been.

His gaze found hers. She quickly pulled the sleeve down, then fiddled with the towel swaddling the baby.

Logan and Manuel carefully and slowly carried Carmen to one of the guest bedrooms. Lily seemed to be everywhere, her smile warm, her manner gentle, making sure the new mother was comfortable. With a broad grin, Ned carried in a cradle. "I made this for Meg when she was born." He winked at her. "I guess you don't remember."

She smiled fondly at the balding man. "I remember putting my dolls in it for their naps."

Lily flicked back a stray strand of hair that had escaped her bun. "I'll get it ready. We found a few baby blankets and kimonos in the attic. I threw them in the washer. We'll be all ready for this little one in no time. Now, how about all of you come down to the kitchen and we'll get some lunch."

Manuel looked worried. "No trouble."

Lily planted her hands on her hips. "Meg, tell him we have to eat. A few more mouths are not a problem."

In Spanish, Meg explained her aunt's philosophy. Manuel didn't look convinced. Doc Jacobs motioned everyone out of the room. "C'mon folks. Let's let mother and baby get some rest. Meg, after lunch I want to go over a few points with you about nursing. You can explain it to Carmen."

Logan watched as Meg said a few last words to the young mother. Then she followed him into the hall.

Standing close to her, he blocked her from going down the steps. "How serious was the injury to your shoulder?"

"It looks worse than it was."

"How bad?" he pressed.

Her back straightened, and she lifted her chin. "Does the sheriff want to know?"

"No. The man wants to know." He wanted to know too badly for his own good. Something about Meg Dawson drew him. Maybe it had to do with them watching a new life enter the world.

Tension hummed between them for a moment— man-woman tension . . . and awareness.

Finally she let out a pent-up breath. "I finished with formal physical therapy in Lynchburg last week, but still do exercises every morning and night. I'll recover completely."

The vulnerability in her eyes told him she might recover physically, but he wondered about the emotional toll the incident had taken. He knew about emotional tolls. First there had been Shelley's accident, then his son's change in behavior . . . now his disappearance.

Logan's job sometimes drew crisis situations like a magnet. But he was used to investigative work or breaking up a brawl in a local tavern. Personal crises were a different matter. He suddenly realized the last thing he ought to do was get involved in Meg Dawson's.

He moved away from her and waited for her to start down the stairs. "I have to get back to the office."

She looked over her shoulder. "You're not staying for lunch?"

It was just a polite question. He didn't hear interest in her voice. Thank goodness. "No. Duty calls."

At the bottom of the steps, she waited for him. "Thanks for your help with Carmen and Manuel."

"No thanks necessary." She was standing close enough to touch, close enough that he could see golden lights in her eyes, close enough that he had to leave now. He stepped away from Meg toward the door. Then he left, unsettled, without saying goodbye. Because if he did, he might decide to stay for lunch, and he wasn't looking for another complication in his life.

Chapter Two

After supper that evening, Meg weeded the flower garden by the front porch. As Lily peered over her shoulder, the older woman said, "I want to plant yellow and orange tulips this year and put pink ones out back."

"They'll look pretty in the spring with the daffodils," Meg responded, her mind on Logan MacDonald, not the flower garden.

Ned pushed himself back and forth on the porch swing, his head covered by a straw hat. "I should go see if Manuel is still tinkering with his truck. Maybe I can learn something."

"Carmen and the baby are napping," Lily replied. "I checked them before I came out."

Meg had looked in on them, too. She'd stood for a long time watching mother and baby, an unfamiliar longing deep inside her.

Suddenly a yellow-striped kitten scampered out from behind a yew and brushed against Meg's leg. She smiled at Leo, a stray she'd found and befriended soon after she'd returned to Willow Valley.

Ned stood and came to the edge of the porch. "A reporter called from the *Willow Valley Courier*. He wanted to do an interview with Manuel and Carmen, but they didn't want to talk to him. They're very private. I told him to call Logan for the details."

Meg glanced at her uncle. "I'm hoping we can convince Manuel to stay for a week or so."

"It's a shame Logan couldn't stay for lunch." Lily cast a quick look at her husband.

"He's a fine man," Ned remarked as if on cue.

"Fine" wasn't quite the way Meg would characterize Logan. Strong. Decisive. Intuitive. "Who's Travis? I heard Doc ask Logan if he'd heard anything about him."

Lily tidied a few strands of hair that always came loose from the chignon at her nape. "Travis is Logan's son. Logan moved his family here about five years ago. From what he's said and I've heard, Travis never liked Willow Valley. Coming from Philadelphia, I guess that was natural. Logan wanted to give him somewhere wholesome to grow up. But Travis wanted none of it."

"So he ran away?"

Lily exchanged a look with her husband. "I think there's more to it than that."

Ned added what he knew. "About a year after they moved, Logan's wife was in an accident and died. It was tough on the boy. Afterward Travis gave Logan quite a few headaches—coming home late, drinking, grades slipping. Logan was at his wit's end and tried to get the boy help. But Travis wouldn't go to the appointments with the counselor. One day about four months ago, he just up and ran off. He's only sixteen, and Logan's worried sick."

"The police are still looking," Lily explained, "and for the first two months, Logan searched for the boy himself as far as Richmond."

Meg sat back on her heels, forgetting about the weeds. "Doc mentioned a private investigator."

Ned grunted. "Logan's trying everything he can to find Travis."

Her heart aching, Meg said, "Logan must be in unbearable pain. Not knowing where his son is, imagining the worst. How does he go on?"

"He's a strong man," Ned answered.

"A good man," Lily added.

Ned pushed his hat back on his head. "Rumor has it Logan's marriage was rocky before Shelley died. But Logan never talks about it."

Meg couldn't forget the look in Logan's green eyes when Doc had asked for news of Travis.

"Are you going to see Logan again?" Her aunt's tone was filled with eager interest.

"What?" Meg asked dropping her gardening trowel.

"Honey, I can read you like a book. You don't ask idle questions."

"Aunt Lily..."

Her aunt laughed. "It would be good for you to get out, go to dinner, date a man."

"You know dating is the furthest thing from my mind."

Lily's smile faded. "I'm worried about you, child. You're not the same person you were before that terrible man shot you."

Most of the time Meg tried not to think about it. She just wanted to get over it. The problem wasn't the shooting. It was the terror, the panic and the trapped feeling that still gripped her sometimes. But she hadn't had a nightmare in over a week. That was progress. "I'm fine, Aunt Lily. You and Uncle Ned and Willow Valley are all I need."

"For now," her aunt pronounced.

Petting Leo, who'd curled in a ball by her knee, Meg decided she wasn't going to ask what her aunt meant. She didn't want to know.

The following morning, Logan drove to the Carlsons' farm. He was curious to see how Manuel and Carmen were faring. He wished he could do something for the young couple, but he knew Manuel wouldn't accept charity.

He was halfway down the lane when he saw Manuel packing the back of his truck. As he drove closer, he saw Meg standing by the open passenger door. She was gesturing to Manuel and speaking fast while Lily and Ned looked on. Logan could guess what was happening.

He parked on the gravel patch beside the blue compact. Climbing out of his car, he heard Meg speaking to Carmen. All he caught were the words *quédese*, "stay," and *unos pocos días*, "a few days." Carmen spoke quickly and gestured to her husband. As Logan approached, he could see the tears in the young woman's eyes.

Stopping beside Meg, he denied the sudden surge of adrenaline rushing through him. "They're leaving," he said, summing up the situation.

"Yes, and they shouldn't. I've talked to Manuel till I'm blue. But he won't listen."

"Has Carmen tried?"

"She says he's the head of the family—he makes the final decision. But, Logan, just look at her! She needs rest and care...at least for a few days. Doc wants to make sure Tomás—that's what they named him—is nursing adequately. But Manuel insists he can't take advantage of our hospitality."

The baby in Carmen's arms wriggled and cried. Carmen looked as if she were close to tears herself.

Meg spoke to her in Spanish. Carmen let her take Tomás. As the baby squirmed, Meg positioned him on her shoulder as naturally as any mother and patted the infant's back. She looked so...beautiful, standing there like that.

Giving himself a mental shake, Logan said, "I suppose Doc is afraid if they leave, Carmen won't seek out proper care if she needs it."

"That, too. But I can't convince Manuel to stay." Meg gently rubbed her chin against the baby's downy black hair.

Logan was gripped by an emotion so strong he knew he had to get away from this woman. "I'll talk to him."

Meg took a quick glance at Logan's broad back as he went to the truck. He'd taken her by surprise when he arrived. She'd never expected he'd come back and check on Carmen and Manuel. Yet maybe with the birth of Tomás, he'd felt involved in their lives, too. It proved one thing about him—he was a caring man.

She could never see Todd caring about this young couple, whether they stayed or left. Why hadn't she seen his selfish streak sooner? Why hadn't she recognized his self-absorption? His story, his career, his needs, always came first. Actually it was an old pattern, one she'd learned with her parents. But finally, at age twenty-nine, she'd realized in time that her needs mattered, too.

Logan called, "Ned, come here a minute."

Meg could hear the low rumble of the men's voices but couldn't tell what they were saying as they walked toward the barn. When they reemerged, they were all smiling. Manuel came over to Meg and Carmen. "We stay. A little while. If I have work." He helped his wife from the cab of the truck.

Carmen squeezed Meg's hand. *"Gracias."*

Meg shook her head. *"No hicenada especial."*

Carmen gazed at Logan. *"Gracias."*

He smiled. *"De nada."*

Meg handed Tomás to the young Mexican woman. Manuel put his arm around her shoulders and guided her back to the house. Lily and Ned followed.

Closing the door of the cab, Meg turned to Logan. "What did you say to him?"

"It was what Ned said. I reminded him of all the machinery that needs a good overhauling and the back field that has to be mowed before winter. Manuel is going to take care of that and, in return for the work, he'll accept room and board for his family."

Meg clasped Logan's arm. "What a wonderful idea!" His skin was hot under hers, the hairs on his forearm rough against her fingers. His green eyes darkened, and her heart raced. She removed her hand.

"Not wonderful. Just expedient. The trading of goods and services. I'm not so sure we shouldn't do it more often." Logan glanced at his watch. "Did you have breakfast?"

She shook her head.

"I'm not officially on duty for a half hour or so. How about going to the bakery with me for a dough-nut and a cup of coffee?" When she hesitated, he added, "I get tired of my own company sometimes. I thought maybe we could just...talk. But if you're too busy—"

"No, I'm not too busy. A cup of coffee sounds good. Aunt Lily makes me herbal tea. Even after all these years, I just can't get used to it."

Logan laughed, a deep, masculine sound that warmed Meg through and through. "She tries to serve it to me when I visit."

"You visit? You haven't since I've been here."

"Yes, well, circumstances the last few months have changed my habits."

Meg saw the pain again. "Aunt Lily told me about your son. I'm sorry."

He shook his head. "Sorrow, blame, regrets. None of it matters except finding Travis. But I don't go on wild-goose chases anymore, driving into the dead of night, speeding down a highway, hoping when I get wherever the road takes me I'll find him. Now I spend my time printing more pictures and flyers, studying the computer data bases, keeping in touch with contacts on other police forces and my private investiga-tor...and working. Working to forget."

Although Meg had always enjoyed her work, she knew about working to forget. She wanted to clasp Logan's arm again, to say she understood, but touching him was dangerous. Doubting he needed her understanding, she nodded toward the house. "I'll make sure Carmen is settled again and meet you at the bakery on Elm. Then you don't have to drive back out here."

The bakery bell tinkled as Meg pulled open the door. Logan sat at one of the five black wrought-iron tables for two. She'd had second thoughts about meeting him, and thirds. Why had she accepted the offer? Because she liked Logan MacDonald, besides feeling attracted to him. If talking could ease his pain concerning his son, she'd listen.

A mug of coffee waited at the empty place across from him, along with two doughnuts and a muffin. Meg couldn't suppress a smile as she sat down. "Do I look underfed?"

His gaze brushed over her quickly. "No. You look just right."

She felt the heat creep up her cheeks again. No other man had ever made her blush. She chose the cranberry muffin and pushed the other pastries toward him. "Aunt Lily tries to feed me constantly. She always has."

"She mentioned a few times that you lived with them when you were a teenager."

Meg had accepted Logan's invitation expecting to talk about him, not about herself. But he was obviously fishing for her background. Picking up her coffee, she took a sip before she said, "My parents are anthropologists. For my first twelve years, I traveled with them most of the time—mainly in Central and South America, but I also spent time with my aunt and uncle. At twelve, I decided I'd rather stay in Willow Valley than globe-trot."

He gazed at her a few moments as if he was trying to see what she wasn't saying. She wasn't even sure herself about all the emotions that surfaced when she thought about those years, when she thought about her parents not wanting her. Even though she'd had her aunt and uncle, she'd still felt abandoned.

Logan added cream to his coffee. He offered one to Meg, and she shook her head. "A purist," he teased.

"What's the point of caffeine if you dilute it?"

He grinned. "On my fourth cup, I find it more palatable. I have a pot sitting in my office all the time." Leaning back in his chair, he broke off half of the doughnut and ate it. "So, at twelve you didn't want to globe-trot, but for your adult life, you have."

"I didn't go into this profession to travel. That just goes along with it sometimes."

He leaned forward again, his hand almost brushing hers as he rested it on the table. "Why did you choose to be an interpreter?"

Instead of touching his large hand, as she wanted to do out of curiosity to see what would happen, she toyed with the paper around her muffin. "Because I wanted to help people understand each other. I had a talent for languages because of my upbringing. I was always amazed by the difference in the way people treat each other when they can understand each other. There's less fear, less anxiety, less suspicion."

He pulled his hand back and wrapped his fingers around his mug. "How many languages can you speak?" His knee briefly touched hers under the table, but he moved his away.

"Four fluently, not counting dialects." She sipped again at her coffee.

"You're uncomfortable talking about yourself, aren't you?"

"I didn't expect to have coffee with you and talk about me."

He smiled. "Why not?"

"Because I thought you might want to talk about Travis."

He went silent and his jaw tensed. If she'd ever seen a man in pain, that man was Logan. She waited.

His voice deeper, his words terse, he responded, "I think about him day and night. Believe me, I don't want to talk about the thoughts that are running through my head. And you don't want to know what they are."

They sat at a stalemate, Meg wondering if Logan kept all his feelings bottled up, not just those about Travis. She understood his need to keep a lid on his emotions. She did the same thing.

Logan's pager beeped, breaking the tension. "Excuse me, I have to make a call."

Meg watched Logan as he went to the phone behind the counter. The calls for him must be a constant source of hope, but disappointment, too. His face remained neutral as he dialed a number. As he began talking, there was a slight change in his stance, and he rubbed the back of his neck. He wasn't getting news of his son—not good news anyway.

When he came back to the table, he said, "I have to cut this short. Cal needs me at the office."

She stood. "I need to get back, too." All of a sudden, Meg knew that getting involved with Logan would be more complicated than being involved with a photojournalist who always considered his career more important than their relationship. She didn't need involvement; she needed peace. As they walked to the door and she said goodbye, she knew the less she saw of Logan the more peaceful she'd feel.

A few days later, Meg picked up the *Willow Valley Courier*. When she saw her own picture on page one, the same picture that had run in newspapers across the country five weeks ago, memories overwhelmed her. By the time she'd finished the article, the numbness had worn off and she was furious.

Logan's comments to the reporter about Manuel and Carmen were strictly factual. But he had included her in the mix. Inadvertently or not, he'd dragged her into their drama. He might be sheriff, but she had a right to her privacy just as Manuel and Carmen did. She sat and fumed for a few minutes, then suddenly decided to tell him how she felt.

Meg drove to the sheriff's department and turned off the ignition before she changed her mind. When she pulled open the door to the office and stepped inside, she saw Cal Martin, one of Logan's deputies, sitting at the front desk.

In a crisp tone, she said, "I'm here to see Sheriff MacDonald."

Cal looked her over. "And your name?"

"Meg Dawson."

Cal's gaze flashed with recognition. He pointed to the closed office in the back. "Just knock on his door."

She could feel Cal's eyes on her back as she crossed the room. Seeing Logan sitting at a massive, scarred wooden desk, she rapped sharply on the glass-paneled door.

He looked up and rose from his chair, opening the door in one quick motion. She'd stood face-to-face with him before, but today his shoulders seemed broader, his legs longer. She should have done this by phone.

"What's the matter, Meg?"

No doubt her color was high. She hadn't bothered to run a brush through her hair, and her old cutoffs and short, sleeveless knit top didn't add to a sense of self-confidence. Boy, she really hadn't thought this through.

She slapped the paper on his desk and her purse on top of it. "That's what's wrong. Why did you mention me and Costa Rica?"

Logan's brows arched. "Everything I told the reporter is a matter of public record. Doc Jacobs delivered Manuel and Carmen's baby boy in Lily and Ned's barn. You acted as interpreter. The reporter was the one who remembered you'd made news before. I just confirmed it."

"Why did you have to mention me at all?"

Her voice had risen with her question. Cal was looking at her and Logan.

Logan firmly clasped her arm and tugged her away from the door so he could close it. "What's going on, Meg?"

Feeling embarrassed for making herself a spectacle, she stepped away from him. "Carmen and Manuel turned down the interview. I certainly wouldn't have agreed to one. This...this—" she waved to the picture "—was unexpected. That's all."

Logan's gaze probed hers until she looked away. She took a few deep breaths, then pushed her hair behind her ear, staring at her picture in the paper, the picture of her and Ramón Pomada standing at the car on the airport runway after the kidnapper had run to the plane. She involuntarily clutched her shoulder, remembering the way it had hurt. She remembered . . .

Logan was close again. "Meg," he said gently, "what are you thinking?"

"I, uh, I guess I shouldn't have bothered you. I should have realized even old news is still news in Willow Valley."

Logan rested his hands on her shoulders. "Have you talked to anyone about what you went through?"

She looked over his shoulder, trying to deny the emotions swelling inside her. "Just the debriefer." Her breaths were coming quicker.

"You weren't allowed to give interviews, were you?"

Her chest tightened, and the air in the room suddenly got thinner. "The governments involved thought it would be better if I didn't. They just gave the facts."

"So why did the rehash of the story bother you now?"

His gentle voice stirred her emotions into chaos, making her feel too vulnerable. "The picture," she murmured as she felt tears prick at her eyes. Now she really felt foolish. She ducked her head and stared straight into Logan's chest. She could see each breath he took, could feel the warmth of his hands on her shoulders. . .and wished she was anyplace else but here.

He tipped her chin up. "It's okay to let it out. If you haven't yet, you're going to have to soon or it will eat at you."

"But I..." She couldn't stop the tears.

He pulled her against his chest. "It's okay," he murmured. "It's okay."

Logan couldn't help but wrap his arms around Meg. Her reaction seemed to have surprised her more than him. He suspected she wasn't used to leaning on anyone. From what she'd said about her childhood, she'd learned at an early age to depend on herself. When he'd invited her to have coffee with him, he'd acted on impulse. He'd found himself thinking about her often, wanting to know more about her, weighing the pros and cons of seeing her again.

Right now she was a woman who needed a shoulder... his shoulder. With his arms around her, her hands pressed against his chest, he wished she could just let go of her ordeal and its effects, but it wasn't that easy. Nothing ever was. He could feel her quick breaths, feel the tension as she resisted his support.

The scent of roses teased Logan, Meg's curves against him felt too right and holding her aroused him. The warmth between them became heat. Her top was a thin barrier as his thumb slipped from the material to her bare skin. His desire grew stronger, and he closed his eyes. Bittersweet pleasure. His life was a mess. She'd go back to her job after Thanksgiving. Even if he wanted just a—

Meg abruptly pulled away, avoided his gaze and reached for her purse. She took out a tissue, blew her nose, then faced him. "I'm sorry."

"There's nothing to be sorry about."

She looked at the file cabinet behind him. "I'm not like this. I don't cry. I don't overreact."

"Do you want to talk about it?"

"I don't even know what to talk about."

"Maybe how terrifying it is to be held hostage?"

She shook her head. "I just want to forget it."

"I've been in the middle of gang wars and drug deals. I understand, Meg, I really do."

She took a deep breath, and he wanted to pull her into his arms again. "Have dinner with me tomorrow night."

"Dinner?" She looked surprised he'd asked.

He'd surprised himself. "Yeah. I'll cook something at my place. And if you want to talk about Costa Rica, you can."

She gave him a weak smile. "And if I don't want to talk about it?"

He could think of something else he'd much rather do than talk, starting with kissing and ending with . . . "If you don't want to talk, you don't have to talk."

She moved closer to the door, but it also brought her closer to him again. "Lily might need my help if Carmen and Manuel are still here."

He thought about stepping away from her, but didn't. "I think she and Ned can handle one evening by themselves. Don't you?"

When Meg slowly nodded, her shiny hair barely brushed her shoulders. It was as natural and free as she was. He wanted to touch her hair, to touch her. Leaning forward, he felt led by a force greater than them both.

She gazed into his eyes and he couldn't help but slip his hand along her neck under her hair and lower his head.

Meg waited for Logan's kiss, thought about it, was eager for it. He'd felt so strong and sturdy and safe as she'd let him hold her. But now, as she gazed into his eyes, she knew he wasn't safe. There was passion there, and yearning and needs only a woman could fulfill for a man. If he kissed her, they'd tap the need—in both of them.

But Logan didn't kiss her. Instead, he removed his hand from under her hair, the touch of his fingers as they slid along her neck leaving a burning heat she wouldn't soon forget. When he raised his head and dropped his hand, she felt a loss of something she suspected would curl her toes.

A slip of a smile turned up one corner of his mouth. With a nod, he gestured to the outer office. Cal stared directly at the two of them through the glass pane.

Logan's tone was wry. "This isn't the most private place in Willow Valley."

She backed away from Logan and picked up her purse on the desk. "Sometimes I wonder if *any* place is private in Willow Valley."

He studied her carefully for a moment. "We'll have privacy tomorrow night."

Flustered, her emotions swirling, not only from what had almost happened with Logan but from the confusion the picture in the paper had stirred up, she moved toward the door. "All right. Can I bring anything?"

He shook his head. "Just yourself."

If she was making a mistake, she'd find out tomorrow night.

Chapter Three

Standing at the door to Logan's house Saturday evening, Meg took a deep breath. The air was getting cooler. September had arrived, and with it the promise of fall. She shifted the bottle of wine to her left arm and rang the doorbell.

A few moments later, Logan opened the door to the brick bi-level. She'd never seen him dressed in anything but his uniform before. He wore a simple white polo shirt, black shorts and Docksides without socks. His thighs were muscled, his legs long, his arms bronzed by the sun. Black hair curled at the V where his two buttons were unfastened. He was sexy and virile, and she was suddenly very nervous.

She handed him the bottle of wine. "I couldn't come empty-handed." His green eyes swept over her, from the gold barrette in her hair, over her emerald culotte dress to her white sandals. When his gaze lingered a moment on her lips, she felt shivers slide up her spine.

Taking the bottle from her, he smiled. "This will be just right. I've barbecued chicken on the grill. I thought we could eat on the deck." Logan motioned her inside. "Come on in."

She followed him up a few stairs to the living room. "Do you have a family room downstairs?"

"I use it for storage. I'm a little short on family right now."

The pain on his face hurt her. He looked as if he were far away somewhere, and she suspected he was thinking about his son. "I'm sorry, Logan. That was thoughtless of me."

When he met her gaze, the pain was still there but controlled now. "You couldn't be thoughtless if you tried."

"You just met me."

"Maybe so. But in my business, I have to read people in an instant sometimes. My life has depended on it."

"Willow Valley must seem tame compared to what you came from."

"It's different. But that's what I wanted when I moved my family here."

Despite how Logan had reacted at the bakery when she'd mentioned Travis, she wouldn't let his son be a taboo subject between them. "Aunt Lily told me Travis wasn't happy here."

"He wasn't. He had his mind set before we came." Logan's curt tone told her he still preferred not to discuss his son.

Meg examined the living room. A gray sofa, streaked with abstract shapes of navy, sat across from an ebony entertainment center. A gray easy chair complemented the sofa. A ladder-backed rocker, two end tables with gray ceramic lights and a coffee table completed the room. But the place still didn't look lived-in.

She crossed to the entertainment center and picked up a framed picture on one of the shelves. A teenage boy stood by the trunk of a maple tree, staring absently across the yard. "Travis?"

Logan nodded.

"He's a handsome young man." He looked a lot like his father.

Logan crossed the room and stood beside her. "He's an unhappy young man."

Meg thought about her own upbringing. "Raising children is complicated."

The silence between them lasted a few moments. Finally Logan said, "You're determined to make me talk about him, aren't you?"

"You need to talk about him, about more than his disappearance."

When Logan raised his hand, she knew he was going to touch her. His fingers on her cheek gave her a thrill of pleasure she'd never known.

His voice was husky when he asked, "How did you get so smart?"

"It doesn't have anything to do with being smart. The heart and the head don't always speak the same language."

He smiled. "I guess the trick is getting them to understand each other."

She nodded and, when his fingers slipped away, she wished he was touching her again. She took the picture with her to the sofa. "Tell me about him."

Logan sat beside her, his knee barely brushing hers. "He's sixteen, thinks he's the smartest kid in the world and is more rebellious and stubborn than any teenager I've ever known."

"He's a junior?"

"Yes. At least he would be if he came home."

"What does he like to do?"

Logan looked at a loss for a moment. "Besides getting in trouble, I don't really know. We haven't had an amicable conversation in a long time."

Logan's expression was full of regret for all that had been. "The last time we talked, he called me his jailor. If he wasn't home by curfew, I'd go out and find him. I think he hated me."

"Logan."

"That's the truth, Meg. And now I can't sleep at night wishing I'd handled everything differently. If I could just find Travis, I'd tell him I don't care if he wears three earrings or torn jeans or shaves his head. I'll even make his curfew an hour later. I just want him home."

Meg reached out and covered Logan's hand. "Doc said the whole town is praying. *Is* there anything else anyone can do?"

He sandwiched her hand between his and gently rubbed his thumb over the tops of her fingers. "No, there's nothing anyone can do except pray."

She stared into his eyes, feeling his pain, feeling his need, drawn to him in an elemental way. Finally Logan cleared his throat and released her hand. "I have the chicken wrapped in foil on the grill. We'd better get to it, or it'll be too dry to eat."

Supper. That's why she was here.

Logan had already set the redwood table. A light breeze stirred the paper napkins under the silverware. Steps led from the deck down to a long yard separated by a spirea hedge from the next-door neighbor's property.

"Is there anything I can do to help?"

"There's a salad in the refrigerator."

Besides the salad, Logan's refrigerator was practically empty. Two bottles of beer, two cans of soda, a hunk of Swiss cheese, the remainder of a head of lettuce and a package of carrots sat on the top shelf. Other than that, his cupboard was bare.

Meg carried the teak salad bowl outside. Logan had just placed the chicken on a platter and unwrapped the foil from two baked potatoes. As she slid onto the bench, he straddled the one on the other side and gave her a quick grin. "I forgot to buy butter at the store. But I have salt and pepper. I don't cook often."

"You don't spend much time here, do you?"

He swung his other leg under the table and raised his head. "No. Is it so obvious?"

"Nothing out of place in the living room, a spotless kitchen. Sure signs."

"I spend most of my time in my office. When I'm hungry, I run up to Gibson's Grocery."

"Chips and cookies?"

"Uh-oh. The lady is on to me."

She smiled. "Quick and filling. I do the same thing when I'm on the run. I get tired of cucumber sandwiches at receptions and hotel food."

"Where's your home base?"

"An apartment in Chevy Chase."

"Are you looking forward to getting back?"

When she was traveling, she did. Her apartment was sunny, comfortable and close to anything she needed. "I'm enjoying my time with Lily and Ned. D.C. and foreign embassies seem a world away."

Logan delved into world affairs with Meg as they ate. He was a stimulating conversationalist, quick to catch her train of thought, a good listener. Her stomach would jump whenever he smiled. His deep voice, lower when he disagreed with her, carried a timbre of authority, yet he listened when she explained her views. They both veered away from personal subjects. That moment in the living room had been too fraught with emotion, too tempting, too dangerous, to explore further, at least right now.

The sun slipped behind the clouds, streaking them and the sky with orange, pink and purple. The passage of time seemed inconsequential as shadows vanished into dusk and fireflies blinked under the maples in the yard.

Suddenly Logan stopped in midsentence. "We forgot the wine. Some host I turned out to be. I set it on the counter, so it's not even chilled."

"Perfect with ice cubes," she teased.

"You *are* kidding."

"Nope."

"All right. I'll be right back."

She called after him, "Just half a glass."

Climbing from the bench, she straightened her belt and wandered to the railing, folding her arms on the weathered wood.

It wasn't long before Meg felt Logan at the back door, watching her. But she didn't turn around. Whenever their gazes connected, the tumult inside her was too unsettling for her to analyze. Out of the cor-

ner of her eye, she could see the glow of the kitchen
light. The door opened and shut, and she found herself holding her breath, which was silly.

At least, she thought it was silly until Logan stood
beside her and offered her a glass of wine. When he
handed her the juice glass, she realized the trembling
inside her extended to her fingers. She took a sip and
set the glass on the balustrade.

He did the same. "We didn't talk about Costa Rica
and what happened to you there." His voice was low,
and in the shadows he seemed almost larger than life.

"It's not necessary, Logan. I'm fine."

"That's a generic word that doesn't describe or explain anything. You're not a generic lady."

Logan made her feel feminine and special. As she
was growing up, tagging along with her parents, she'd
often felt she was a bother. She'd thought she'd put all
that behind her—the feelings of loneliness and isola-
tion. Costa Rica had stirred them up, and being cared
for and loved by Lily and Ned hadn't eased them but
had brought even more confusion to the surface. And
now Logan, making her feel she was special . . .

"Meg?"

Even in the darkness, her eyes sought his. Connected to him for the moment, she felt the impact of
her loneliness, more loneliness than she'd ever felt before.

Logan stroked her hair away from her cheek, and
she trembled. When he bent his head, she knew she
wanted his kiss and needed his kiss. But panic rose
within her. In an instant, she realized she was as afraid
of involvement with Logan as she was of returning to
her profession.

Afraid? Of doing the work she loved? Why?

The questions alarmed her almost as much as the thought of drowning in Logan's embrace. She pulled away from him, confused and afraid, but not sure of what.

"I have to go, Logan." Her voice was firm although her insides were quivering like jelly. *Always keep an outwardly calm appearance. Always hide personal feelings. Always smile and act gracious.* She'd learned to hide her feelings from her parents, and her profession reinforced her inner rules. Often she had to hide her thoughts while she conveyed someone else's words. But she didn't want to think about it now; she just wanted to escape.

Logan didn't mention the almost-kiss. But he did confront her. "What's wrong?"

"Nothing's wrong. It's getting late, and Lily and Ned will worry."

"You're a big girl, Meg."

She summoned up a smile. "Lily forgets that."

"You don't have to run off just because we were getting a little too intense."

Intense. Yes, and turned-on, too. Ignoring his statement, she plowed on as if he were a foreign diplomat and she were his interpreter. "Thank you so much for dinner. I enjoyed it."

Logan frowned. "I did, too. Maybe we can do it again sometime."

Not until she straightened out her thoughts. Not until she knew what was scaring her so. She nodded and went to the door. "I can let myself out. Really, Logan, I had a lovely time."

She reached for the door, and he didn't move. Maybe he realized if he came toward her, she'd run even faster.

"Tell Lily and Ned I'll stop by soon," Logan said in a low voice, reminding her she couldn't run from him forever. "I want to see Manuel, Carmen and the baby again before they leave."

Opening the door, she stepped into the kitchen. "I will. Thanks again for supper."

Meg let the door shut behind her. Logan didn't follow her, and she told herself she was glad. But when she reached her car and turned on the ignition, she wondered how different the night might have been if he had.

The morning was clear, the sky blue, the air carrying the lingering fragrance of the last days of summer. Meg had decided to walk to Willow Valley high school Monday morning for her appointment with the principal instead of driving. She needed the time alone to think.

After she'd left Logan's apartment Saturday night, she'd returned to Lily and Ned's and sat on the porch in the old wooden swing. For the first time in a long time, she'd remembered the conversation she'd overheard when she was twelve. The conversation that had changed her life.

"Meg was an accident that never should have happened," her mother said to her father. "But everything has worked out. She's only held us back a few times. If she decides to stay with Lily while we go to Calcutta, that's her choice. She's old enough to make it."

At that moment Meg had realized she *was* old enough to make a choice and decide what was best for her. She would stay with her aunt and uncle permanently while her parents traveled, and accept the love her Aunt Lily and Uncle Ned could offer—because her parents apparently had none to give.

Swinging and staring at the moon last night long after midnight, she understood why she was afraid to get involved with Logan. When she was a child and her parents left her at her aunt and uncle's while they traveled, she'd learned that attachment hurt. Loving her parents, wanting their love in return, she'd discovered abandonment hurt even worse. Nurtured by Lily and Ned, she'd missed them when she traveled with her parents. But staying at Lily and Ned's, she'd longed to be with her parents. The situation was confusing for a child. At twelve she'd tried to end the confusion by staying in Willow Valley.

When she was an adult, her relationship with Todd had just reinforced the fact that attachment led to hurt. She'd made friends in D.C. But they were social friends, not friends in whom she'd confide. She'd never confided in Todd, either, not about her deepest feelings and dreams. Yet she'd let Logan see a vulnerable side of her she usually kept hidden. She could still feel his arms around her, the brush of his fingers against her cheek. Her attraction to Logan had taken her by surprise. Yet she could cope with that. After all, she didn't have to be around him. She didn't want to get involved, so she'd simply stay away. The solution to that problem was easy.

But her career and her fear of returning to D.C. were another matter. She loved her work. It was important and necessary. Yet she was scared that she'd be put in a situation again where her interpretation skills could be a matter of life and death. She was afraid of the responsibility, afraid of getting hurt again, but most of all, afraid of making a mistake. She could have cost everyone involved their lives. It was her fault that their kidnapper had started shooting. Thank God she was the only one who'd gotten hurt. But what about the next time? What if...?

Meg hurried across the parking lot of the high school, trying to chase her thoughts away. Entertaining doubts would only give them more power. She swung open the door to the building and headed for the office. The lobby had a familiar wax-and-chalk smell, and she smiled. During her time in high school, living with her aunt and uncle, she'd finally experienced a sense of belonging and stability that had been missing from her first twelve years.

When Meg opened the door to the office and stepped inside, the secretary smiled at her. "Can I help you?"

"I have an appointment with Michael Holden at eleven-thirty."

The door to the principal's office stood open. Meg heard two masculine voices. In fact, if she wasn't mistaken...

Michael stood in the doorway and motioned to her to come into his office. He was six feet tall and in his late thirties. He'd accepted the position as principal of Willow Valley high school the year before. Lily had introduced Meg to the man after church services one Sunday. Meg didn't know much about him—just that his blue eyes twinkled when he smiled and his voice was gentle yet strong enough to persuade recalcitrant teenagers to listen to him. He'd written to her, asking her to consider participating in an assembly for the students. She'd made this appointment with him to discuss it.

Except she hadn't expected to see Logan Mac-Donald standing in the principal's office. In his uniform, he always seemed to be taller, broader, a force she couldn't ignore.

Logan stared directly at her, as if he were trying to see something inside. "I had a meeting with Michael this morning. He's organized a local parents' group that will go to work as soon as a child is lost or missing."

The Sheriff was making it clear his presence here had nothing to do with her. Without waiting for a response from her, he said to Michael, "I'll call you after I've spoken with my P.I. again. Meg, I'll see you soon."

His tone was cool and polite, reserved in a way it hadn't been before. But she knew it was better for both of them if they limited contact. After all, she'd be going back to D.C. eventually. She focused her attention on Michael Holden and the program she wanted to present to his students.

Logan left the school, fully intending to drive back to his office. But once in his car, he didn't put the key in the ignition. All he could think about was Meg Dawson—the way they'd connected, the way she'd left his house so abruptly, the way she'd stood in Michael Holden's office, a wall surrounding her. Something had spooked her. And damn if he wasn't going to find out exactly what it was.

He examined the visitors' parking places and didn't see a blue compact car. It was possible Meg had walked to the school. Ned and Lily's place was about a mile away. Logan checked his watch every five minutes. Finally the sun blazing in his windshield urged him to get out of his car.

Twenty minutes later, Meg pushed open the door of the lobby and stepped outside. The sun shone on her brown hair, making blond strands glow. The gold buttons on her red sailor blouse gleamed. Her red skirt molded to her legs as a warm breeze blew.

Logan slid behind the wheel, shut his door and started the car. He moved on instinct rather than logic. Before Meg stepped off the curb, he'd driven in front of the entrance, reached across and opened the passenger door.

Her expression showed her surprise. "What are you still doing here?"

"I decided to take my lunch break and give you a ride home. You don't have your car, do you?"

"No, but..."

He appraised her, from her silky brown hair to her sandals. "And you certainly don't need the exercise, so hop in."

"Logan, I don't need a chauffeur."

"Of course you don't. And I don't want to be one. Hop in anyway. We need to talk."

"Logan, really..."

"Miss Dawson, we're soon going to cause a scene if you don't get in. Because I'm not leaving without you."

She looked thoroughly frustrated with him as she slid inside, then slammed the door.

It was clear that whatever talking he wanted to do, he'd have to initiate. He pulled his car out onto the two-lane road and headed towards Lily and Ned's. "Tell me what happened Saturday night."

"Nothing happened."

"I don't see you as a woman who hides behind denial. You're too intelligent for that."

Meg stared out the windshield. "I've solved my own problems for a very long time. I'm not about to depend on someone else to do it now."

"So there *is* a problem."

"Let it go, Logan. Life's like a puzzle. You just have to figure out how to fill in the pieces so they fit."

He glanced at her profile. "Your philosophy?"

"Uncle Ned's."

Meg was making it very clear she wanted him to butt out of her life. And he should. Their roads wound in different directions.

After he cruised down the lane to the farm, he got out of the car quickly and went around to Meg's side. She'd already opened the door. When she climbed out, she stood beside him looking nervous.

He was feeling a bit jittery himself, unsettled by the inner turmoil he felt whenever he was close to her. "I understand if you don't want someone to problem-solve for you. But if you need to talk, I can listen."

When she looked up at him, he wanted to kiss her. But he knew he'd scare her away. So instead, he gently tapped the tip of her nose. "You know where to find me."

It was hard for him to leave her there, to drive away without another word. He'd give her some time. If she didn't come to him, he'd be back to find out why she was afraid of him . . . of them together.

The terror. She could still feel terror. She was cold . . . so cold. Despite the heat. Despite the perspiration. She interpreted their kidnapper automati-

cally. But her teeth were chattering, she hadn't slept for three days and she was scared...scared she'd say or do something wrong. Think something wrong and put it into words.

The terrorist rattled off his demands. She conveyed what he wanted to the official on the phone. Suddenly their kidnapper shouted and waved his gun. Pomada yelled. Meg didn't know what she'd said wrong. But she moved toward the man, hoping to reassure him—

He shot.

The searing pain brought her to her knees. No one helped her. She knew Pomada was afraid he'd get shot, too. She reached out anyway. No one reached back. Her ears rang, and dots floated in front of her eyes, turning everything to gray. She couldn't pass out...she couldn't...she couldn't....

Meg awoke, drenched in sweat, the terror as real as it had been that day weeks ago. When would the nightmares stop? When would she forget?

Sunday afternoon, Meg drove to Logan's house, not sure she was doing the right thing. But maybe Logan *was* the one person who could help her. Maybe he'd understand her fear of going back to work. She needed someone else's perspective. Logan himself had said he'd experienced traumatic situations. How did he make himself do it again? How did he persuade himself to take the same risks or face the same challenges when he'd narrowly escaped injury before?

Meg rang Logan's doorbell, not wanting him to solve her problem but hoping he'd share his experience. When he didn't answer the door, she rang the bell again and reminded herself she was here to talk about her work, not to satisfy her curiosity about her attraction to him.

Both the sheriff's car and Logan's sedan sat in the driveway. The garage door was open, so he had to be around. She descended the porch steps and followed the path around the side of the house. A low buzzing became louder as she rounded the corner. Logan was using a hedge trimmer on the spirea. His bare back, tanned and muscled, gleamed with sweat in the bright sun.

Because of the buzz of the trimmer, he couldn't hear her as she walked toward him. She stared at the strong column of his neck, his hair damp and wavy on his nape, his straight spine, his denim cutoffs riding low on his hips. The sparks inside Meg flicked against her warning to herself, threatening to ignite with a matching response from Logan.

Suddenly he turned around.

She stopped and took a deep breath. But that didn't help because she inhaled sun and male, potent enough to make her head spin.

Logan's stare was intense, then he smiled. "I wasn't expecting company."

Her gaze went straight to his chest—a broad chest covered by black hair. A mat of it whorled around his dark male nipples then arrowed down the center, disappearing under the snap of his shorts. Meg felt herself getting hotter the longer she stared. "I, uh, thought I'd ask about your perspective."

"On ... ?"

"What happened to me in Costa Rica. There's something you don't know."

He came closer. Her fingers tingled, and she realized she wanted to touch him. There was no point denying it.

"Why don't you sit on the deck while I shower? Then we can talk."

Meg went up the stairs to the deck and settled in a lawn chair while Logan wound up the cord to the hedge trimmer. He climbed the steps and opened the door, his gaze lingering on her. "I'll just be a few minutes."

She heard the underlying message. He didn't want her to run away. As he went inside, she closed her eyes. She'd never been afraid of life or the challenges it presented. But right now she felt like running far away and hiding. She made herself sit still and wait.

Not ten minutes later, Logan opened the screen door. "Iced tea or soda?"

"Iced tea."

He gave her a smile that made her knees wobble although she was sitting.

She heard the ring of the phone in the kitchen and Logan's deep rumble as he answered it. A few seconds later, he came outside, his expression grim. "That was a hospital in Richmond. Travis was mugged."

Chapter Four

Logan's expression reflected a mixture of dismay, relief and worry.

Meg couldn't keep herself from going to him. "How is Travis? Are his injuries serious?"

Logan raked his fingers through his hair and shook his head. "Cuts and bruised ribs. A black eye. They kept him overnight for observation. He only gave them my number now because his doctor threatened him with the juvenile authorities if he didn't. They wouldn't release him on his own."

Meg knew the drive to Richmond would take about three hours. She could imagine Logan's concern, recriminations and hope as he drove. "Would you like me to go along?"

His green eyes gentled, then darkened with the same intensity that had been there right before she'd evaded his kiss. "I'd like that."

An hour later, Meg sat beside Logan as he drove and wondered if she should have offered to come along. She'd called Lily so her aunt wouldn't worry. But Logan had been silent ever since they'd gotten into the car. Meg felt as if she was intruding.

Suddenly he glanced at her. "I'm sorry I'm such lousy company."

"I understand."

He grunted. "No, I'm afraid you don't. You'll probably wish you'd stayed in Willow Valley. Travis can be . . ." Logan sighed.

"Are you afraid he won't want to come home with you?"

Logan adjusted his sun visor with a snap. "I *know* he won't want to come home."

"Even after what he's probably been through?"

"I told you he hates me, Meg. And maybe he has good reason."

"Logan!"

"He's never said it, but he thinks his mother's accident was my fault. And I'm not so sure it wasn't. We had a serious argument. Travis came home just as she raced out of the house. An hour later, she was dead."

Meg didn't know what to say to ease Logan's pain and guilt. "Have you talked to him about it?"

"Since that night, he's pulled away. Now I'm not sure all the talking in the world will help."

Meg could feel Logan's torment. He wanted to love his son, but he thought his son no longer loved him. Meg knew what it felt like not to have love returned. Love was more than saying words. It was a bond that transcended arguments and misunderstandings.

But not abandonment.

As long as Logan kept trying to communicate with his son, trying to reach him, that bond would live. Somehow she had to explain that to Logan. "I didn't know how to talk to my parents. They were so far above me."

He glanced at her. "What do you mean?"

"Their concerns were lofty. They cared about the history of civilization and their research, not about what I'd learned about basket weaving from a native girl my own age, or about the friendship we developed. They met my physical needs—they made sure I was safe. But a child needs more than that."

"I couldn't even keep Travis safe."

Meg could imagine the feelings of responsibility as a parent—the immensity of protecting a child, guiding him on the right path. "Maybe if you talk to him about why he ran away..."

"If I know Travis, he won't be in a talking mood."

"There's always tomorrow."

"If I can chain him down," Logan muttered.

A few minutes later, he switched on the tape player, and classical music filled the car. But as they drove closer to Richmond, the tension increased. Meg wanted to reassure Logan in some way, but didn't know how. She was much too aware of his foot going from the brake to the accelerator, his large hands on the steering wheel, the curling black hair on his forearm and wrist, his tan skin. He drew her gaze again and again. Whenever she peeked at his profile, her stomach fluttered. His rich black hair was cut close to the nape. The lines around his eyes hinted at his forty years, but his strong cheekbones and his determined jaw gave his face vitality and power that wouldn't diminish with age.

He'd shaved when he'd showered. Meg could smell spice, not strong, just part of his scent. Yes, she was too aware of everything about Logan MacDonald. She had been since the first moment she'd felt his presence in her aunt and uncle's barn.

Logan followed signs to the hospital in Richmond. After he parked, he came around to the passenger side and opened Meg's door. She stepped out, and he gave her a wry smile.

They entered the hospital, and Logan halted in the lobby. "The doctor gave me Travis's room number. Would you like to wait here?"

Meg preferred activity to inactivity. "I'd rather come along if you don't mind."

"I don't mind. But I don't know what Travis's attitude will be."

She smiled, hoping to ease Logan's tension. "I'm not afraid of sticky situations. I get involved in them often."

He smiled back. "I guess you do. I keep forgetting you're a professional woman who's been around the world a few times."

"Forget?"

His gaze caressed her face. She could feel it and knew he wanted to touch her. "When I'm with you, I only think about the here and now."

She knew what he meant. It was scary. With Logan, she felt different. Yesterday and tomorrow seemed faraway. The feeling wasn't only scary; it was also dangerous.

If she turned the conversation back to Travis, she could ignore the tugging she felt toward Logan. "What floor is Travis on?"

Logan's eyes remained the same deep green. He knew exactly what she was doing. "Five." When he broke eye contact and nodded toward the elevators, she walked ahead of him, knowing if he touched her, the tugging would become stronger.

They found Travis's room easily. Logan paused outside the door, his jaw set, his forehead creased with concern. Then he strode in, as if he belonged in the hospital, as if he belonged in his son's room.

Travis was dressed, sitting in a chair by the window flipping through a magazine. The sleeve of his shirt sported a long tear, and the denim of his jeans hung in strips over his knees. His school jacket lay across the back of the chair. The right side of his face was swollen, and his right eye was as black and blue as it could be. Meg saw Logan take a deep breath and realized how difficult it was for him to see his son in this condition.

The teenager looked up when he heard footsteps. Meg glimpsed fear in his eyes, relief and, an instant later, defiance.

Logan stood before his son. "How are you?"

"Just fine, Dad. Can't you tell?"

Logan frowned. "I can tell you've gotten yourself into a mess of trouble. Are you ready to come home?"

Travis grunted. "I don't have any choice." He looked over at Meg. "Who's she?"

"This is Meg Dawson."

Coming closer to Travis Meg extended her hand. "Hi."

Travis scowled at his father. "Seems like you've been busy while I've been gone."

"Travis . . ." The anger in Logan's tone was evident.

Meg dropped her hand. "Have *you* been busy, Travis?"

The sixteen-year-old looked at her curiously, then dropped his gaze. "Yeah. I sure have. Enough to know I want to be on my own."

"That's impossible until you're eighteen," Logan snapped. "You don't even have a job."

"Maybe I'll get one. Maybe as soon as I get some money, I'll leave again."

Logan looked as if he wanted to shake some sense into his son. "You try it, and I'll be more of a warden than I've ever been."

"You mean you'll lock me in my room? You might as well."

Meg saw the distress Logan was trying to hide. She saw him try to make himself relax, and she knew his next words were a real effort. "Do you know how worried I've been?"

Travis's expression didn't change, and he didn't respond. Instead, he said, "You have to sign release forms out at the desk before we can go."

Logan tried to hide his pain. "All right. I won't be long."

Travis watched Logan leave, closed the magazine and stared out the window.

"I only met your dad a short time ago, Travis, but I know he *has* been worried."

The teenager looked at her then, as if assessing her. Meg let him study her. Finally he asked, "So how did you meet Dad? Did he stop you for speeding or something?"

She knew he was goading her on purpose. Instead of becoming combative, she asked, "Do you know Ned and Lily Carlson?"

Travis nodded.

"They're my aunt and uncle. I lived with them on and off when I was growing up. I'm back for a visit."

Travis grimaced. "Why would you want to visit Willow Valley? There's nothing there."

"My aunt and uncle are there, and I love them."

"It's a one-horse town."

"Were you any happier in Richmond?" she asked softly.

His tone turned defensive. "I was on the streets. If I had my own place, it would be a lot better than Willow Valley."

Her questions for him came from a deep place inside her. She'd never known a real home, and she wondered why he was so anxious to run away from his. "Would it? Or would you get tired of it the same way you got tired of Willow Valley?"

He took his jacket from the back of the chair. "I never liked Willow Valley. It wasn't my choice to move there."

"Did you give it a chance?" she asked quietly.

He remained silent and slung his jacket over his arm.

"Sometimes it's not the place that matters but the people there or the work."

He studied her curiously. "So what do you do?"

"I'm an interpreter."

She'd apparently piqued his interest. "Where do you usually live?"

"Washington, D.C."

Travis's eyes widened, and he looked impressed.

Logan came back into the room. "Everything's set. Are you ready?"

"As ready as I'm going to be," Travis mumbled.

Logan frowned and waited for Travis to stand. The teenager held his ribs. Logan moved forward, then stopped. The expression on Travis's face told him to stay clear.

If Meg thought the trip *to* Richmond was tense, the trip home couldn't be described. Logan asked his son questions about where he'd been, what he'd been doing, and Travis sullenly mumbled a few monosyllables. The muscle working in his jaw, his hands taking a stranglehold on the wheel, Logan gave up and drove.

An hour from Willow Valley, they passed a few fast-food restaurants. At a red light, Logan asked his son, "Are you hungry?"

"Maybe."

"Yes or no, Travis." Meg could tell Logan was at the end of his patience.

"Go ahead and stop. I don't care where."

Logan pulled into the next fast-food restaurant.

The silence at the table was deafening as Travis devoured two deluxe burgers and a large order of fries. After a slurp of his milk shake, he checked out Meg again. "Do you travel much with what you do?"

"Quite a bit. I have albums full of pictures. In fact, I'm going to be giving workshops at your high school on some of the places I've seen."

"Yeah?" There was a gleam of interest in his eyes, the same green as Logan's.

"Your principal and I have been discussing the best way to do it. Probably through social-studies classes. What do you think I can do so I don't bore everyone?"

Travis shrugged. "Dunno."

Logan frowned.

Meg didn't give up. "What would make it interesting for you?"

The teenager thought for a while. "Not just a slide show. But talking about something neat that happened each place."

Travis had a point. She didn't want to do a travelogue or a lecture. Getting the kids involved would work the best. "I'll have to think about that. If you come up with any ideas, let me know."

His expression was doubtful.

"I mean it."

Travis settled back in his seat with his milk shake.

Logan leaned forward as if physical closeness would bridge the distance between him and his son. "We'll have to go see Mr. Holden and find out what you have to make up from the end of last year. Maybe you could do some independent study and join the rest of your class."

"I'm not sure I want to go back to school."

"You don't have any choice."

"I'm sixteen. I can quit."

"No, you can't. I'll personally escort you every morning if I have to," Logan said with a sternness Meg had never heard from him.

Travis slammed his cup on the table. "Nothing changes, does it? You expect me to do what *you* want."

"I expect you to do what's best for your future. And you will."

"I'll say. Maybe I'll take off again."

Logan stared directly into his son's eyes. "Think about it, Travis, and so help me I'll put you in a military academy so fast your head will spin."

"You'd have to catch me first."

"Do you want me to put a personal bodyguard on you so I know where you are every minute?"

"You wouldn't dare!"

"Try me." Logan's voice was deep with authority and intent.

The two males stared at each other, silently engaged in war. Meg took a deep breath. If someone didn't intercede, they'd do irreparable harm to their relationship.

Laying her hand lightly on Logan's arm, she said to Travis, "You know where Lily and Ned live, don't you?"

Travis blinked and turned toward her. She'd given him an excuse to break eye contact with his father first. "Yeah, I know."

"Stop by sometime, and I'll show you the latest pictures I had developed. If you don't like Willow Valley, you'll probably want to travel some day."

"Some day soon."

She felt Logan's arm tense under her hand. "It's good to have an idea of where you'd like to go, what kind of work is available in those countries—if you're planning to leave the States."

"I'd like to backpack through Spain," he said as if he'd given it lots of thought.

"Do you speak Spanish?"

"I've had two years."

"The best way to learn is to live among the people," she advised.

Logan tried to remain calm, realizing he'd better stay out of the conversation if he wanted to hear what his son had to say. He never knew Travis wanted to backpack through Spain. What else didn't he know? What would Travis let him discover? Nothing had changed between them. It tore Logan up to look at his son. The bruised face, eye, his gaunt cheeks. He'd lost about ten pounds. All Logan wanted to do was to keep his son in Willow Valley until he was mature enough to make his own decisions. He'd do it with a gentle hand or an iron hand. Whatever it took.

In the parking lot, Travis slammed the car door as he settled in the back seat. Logan opened Meg's door. Her elbow brushed his arm as she slid in, and his pulse sped up.

Meg.

She shouldn't be distracting him now. All of his thoughts should center on Travis—what he'd put himself through, what could be done to keep him from running again. But Logan was stumped when it came to his son. And maybe he was letting Meg distract him because her presence was welcome. She was optimistic, insightful and so damn pretty his body tightened every time he looked at her or smelled her perfume or saw her smile.

As he drove the last stretch toward Willow Valley, he wished he knew what to say to Travis. He wished he knew what to say to Meg to tell her how much he appreciated her company today, how much he appreciated her attempts to reach his son. Trouble was, he wasn't sure anyone could get through to Travis.

Back in Willow Valley, Logan pulled into his driveway and pressed the garage-door opener. As soon as the car stopped, Travis got out and disappeared through the garage. A light went on in the house.

Logan leaned his head against the headrest for a moment, letting his emotions settle, trying to tell himself tomorrow would be a better day.

Meg touched his arm. Her fingers were light as if she was hesitant to disturb him. "Is there anything I can do to help?"

He managed a weak smile. "Not unless you have a ton of patience in your pocket you can lend me."

"I wish I did."

He turned his head toward her, surprised by the tenderness he felt for Meg already. She pulled back her hand, and he was sorry she did. He liked her touch. He liked everything about her.

She unsnapped her seat belt, and Logan did the same. By the time he walked around to her side, she'd climbed out and closed the car door. They walked slowly side by side to her car.

He opened the door for her. "Thank you for coming along today."

"I wasn't much help."

The stars seemed to be reflected in Meg's eyes. "You were more help than you know. At least Travis talked to you."

"It's not all your fault," she said softly with so much conviction he almost believed her.

"I've done so many things the wrong way."

"Even parents who do everything right have problems with their children."

"Don't try to ease my conscience, Meg. The move and Shelley's death were hard on him. I should have listened to him more."

"You still can."

"If he'll give me the chance. When we're separated, I have hopes. When we're together..." Logan rubbed the back of his neck. "But he's home. Right now that's what matters. I talked to his doctor at the hospital. He said Travis needs to take it easy for a few days, but he should be fine.''

Meg tilted her head up and smiled. ''He's safe tonight.''

''Thank God. And thank you. I appreciate your support.''

Their gazes locked. They seemed to lean toward each other at the same moment. Logan needed to thank her with more than words. Just a thank-you. That was all. A simple thank-you.

But the instant his lips touched Meg's, he knew nothing would be simple with her. Her caring, her kindness, the quiver in her body when his heat met hers told him they were dangerous together. She was understanding and softness, loveliness and intelligence—a woman who could bring richness to his life.

He pushed his tongue between her lips, hungry for her, yearning for something he couldn't name. He thought she might resist. Maybe he even hoped she'd pull away so he wouldn't have to decide between fair and right, restraint or abandon. But she didn't pull away. She let him taste her, and she tasted him.

This kiss wasn't a thank-you. It was passion as complex as his life. His body surged toward hers. He shuddered as their hips met and he felt her breasts against his chest. The scent of her was as intoxicating as her taste. His fingers closed over tendrils of her hair, sliding into its silkiness. He heard her moan and he caressed her back, stopping at her waist, rocking his hips against hers.

Part of him waited for a protest. Shelley had been a practical lover. She'd taken and given what was necessary, nothing more. But Meg didn't protest. Her hands moved from his shoulders to his neck. She stroked his jaw, and his passion burned even stronger with her touch. He ached to lay her down on the grass and—

Travis was home. Logan had to find out what his son needed and give it to him. He wasn't free to start a relationship with anyone—not when Travis was so unsettled, not when Logan wasn't sure of his abilities as a father, let alone a husband. Shelley's decision to continue to use birth-control pills without telling him had left him wondering what kind of husband he'd been. How many nights when sleep was beyond his grasp had he analyzed their marriage, analyzed his career, his actions, his words, looking for the answer to what he'd done wrong?

He'd married Shelley because it had been the right thing to do. He'd moved his family to Willow Valley so Travis could grow up in the right atmosphere— without danger lurking on every corner. And now...

Travis wanted to run, and Logan couldn't seem to fit the pieces back together again. What business did he have kissing Meg Dawson as if he'd never kiss again? What business did he have involving her in his life when involvement would only bring them both chaos?

She had a life in Washington, D.C. Willow Valley was only a stopping-over point for her. It wasn't home.

As much as his blood raged with the desire to kiss more deeply, touch more intimately, make love with her until confusion was only a memory, he knew better. He was stronger than his desire, more reasonable than a drive that could only cause them both a pack of trouble. He had enough of that already.

He pulled away and opened his eyes. He'd been lost in Meg, lost, for a few minutes, to the reality around him. She opened her eyes, too. He saw the passion still lingering, her surprise that the kiss was over and vulnerability he had no right to see.

But she was quick—quicker than he was. Dropping her hands to her sides, she took a deep breath, then said, "It's been an emotional day, and we're both tired."

As if that explained it all. Could she dismiss the kiss so easily? Could he? He had no choice. "I have to go to Travis."

She nodded. "I know."

Worried about Travis all day, he'd forgotten why Meg had come to him in the first place. "Earlier today, you said you wanted my perspective on Costa Rica. We never got to it."

She shrugged. "I'll work it out."

He clasped her shoulder. "You don't have to work it out alone."

"I always work out my problems alone."

The frustration of the day and the potency of their kiss made him swear. "Dammit, Meg. You don't have to. You gave me moral support today. Can't you see I'd like to do the same for you?"

She took a step back. "You don't owe me anything. And I don't need moral support. Just forget I mentioned Costa Rica."

Maybe she was acting defensive and remote because the kiss had shaken her, too. "The same way I should forget about that kiss?" he pressed.

She didn't hesitate. "Yes."

He touched the back of his hand to her cheek. "You're still flushed. I don't think you can forget it so easily."

Her voice trembled slightly as she asked, "Can you?"

He shook his head. "No. But like you, I'm going to try. If you decide you do need moral support, call me. I'll be glad to listen."

As she stepped away, he knew she wouldn't call. That kiss had changed everything between them. That kiss had pulled them closer together, yet pushed them further away. When she got into her car, he found he was angry at himself, angry with her, but most of all angry at fate. Timing was everything. And the timing for him and Meg was all wrong.

Chapter Five

Pulling a chocolate cake out of the oven Wednesday afternoon, Meg took an appreciative whiff as she set it on a cooling rack. Her uncle loved chocolate cake, and Lily baked one once a week. But today her aunt had complained about feeling tired. Meg had convinced her to nap while *she* baked the cake. Carmen and the baby were sitting in the backyard under the shade of a maple, watching her husband mow the plot of grass on the side of the house.

When Meg looked out the kitchen window, she caught a glimpse of her uncle as he disappeared inside the garage. She couldn't help but smile. Just this morning, he'd patted her head as if she were twelve and told her to enjoy her day. He and her aunt took pleasure from such small things, like their vegetable garden, taking walks by the stream, sitting together on

the front porch, talking with Carmen and Manuel.
Meg sighed. It was a life she might never know.

The doorbell interrupted her reverie. She placed the
pot holders on the counter and went to the living
room. To her surprise, Travis stood at the door, looking unsure. He wore jeans, an oversize T-shirt and a
baseball cap. His face was flushed, and he looked hot.

"Hi, Travis. It's good to see you." She opened the
wooden screen door.

He stuffed his hands into his pockets. "You said to
stop by sometime if I wanted to look at your pictures."

"Sure. Come on in."

He looked agitated as he removed his hands from
his pockets and shifted on his worn sneakers. "I didn't
know if you meant it. I mean, if you're busy or something..."

"I'm not busy. The photographs are right over there
on the coffee table. Would you like some lemonade?"

"Yeah. That'd be great. I walked over, and it's
kinda hot."

She gestured to the sofa. "Make yourself comfortable. I'll be right back."

Meg poured two glasses of lemonade and glanced at
the cake. Crossing to the archway, she asked, "Would
you like a piece of chocolate cake? It's still warm, and
I didn't ice it yet...."

"I don't care about icing. But..." As he trailed off,
his gaze was probing. "Why are you being so nice to
me? Because you're after my dad?"

So that was the real reason for this visit. Meg picked
up the lemonade and went to the couch. She set one
glass on the coffee table for him and took the other

with her to the rocker across from it. "I told you I've only known your dad for a short while."

Travis sat on the edge of the sofa. "That's all it takes."

Meg couldn't lie to Travis. She certainly wasn't "after" Logan, but she couldn't deny the attraction between them that Travis probably sensed. "I admire your dad. We were thrown into an unusual situation together. Did he tell you about Manuel and Carmen?"

Travis shook his head. "He only lectures me. He doesn't talk to me."

Briefly Meg told Travis about the birth of the baby.

The teenager still seemed wary. "But you came with him to get me."

"For moral support."

"Dad doesn't need moral support," Travis argued. "He's a rock." Travis sounded almost sorry, as if he wished Logan weren't so strong.

"He was worried about you, relieved he knew where you were, but concerned about your injuries."

The boy stared at the stack of photographs. "Yeah, so concerned he's making me go to school tomorrow."

It was obvious Travis needed someone to talk to, someone who wouldn't either judge or dismiss him. "You feel you need more time? Are your ribs still bothering you?"

He flushed. "No. It's just . . . it's going to be hard seeing everyone after being gone. But dad told me if I get decent grades this year, he'll buy me a used car next summer. He called it a contract, and if I screw up I don't get the car. I know it's a bribe to get me to do what he wants."

"What do *you* want?"

Travis met her gaze directly with the same honesty she'd found in Logan. "I don't know. I feel trapped here."

Somehow she wanted to help him see his options so he could start living life instead of running away from it. "Can you look at getting your diploma as the key to freedom?"

He looked puzzled for a moment. "You really believe that?"

"Yes. Without it, you *will* be trapped. With it, new worlds will open up to you, and you can choose whichever one you want. You mentioned backpacking in Spain. Did you ever consider becoming an exchange student for a semester?"

"No. I never even thought I could."

Smiling, she suggested casually, "I bet if you ask Mr. Holden, he'll find information for you. But it would depend on your grades whether you're eligible or not."

Travis picked up his glass and took some long swallows. Then he set it down with a click. "So, if you're not after my dad, why do you care? I'm nothing to you."

"I guess because I relate to how you feel. I know it makes a difference if you have a goal, if you're heading toward something rather than running away from something, whether it be your parents or a small town or a life you don't want."

Travis turned his lemonade glass around on the table and stared at the top photograph on the stack, a shot of the Jefferson Memorial. "So, what was *your* goal? If you like it here, why don't you stay?"

Meg had thought about that ever since she'd graduated from college. "Because I traveled so much as a child, I had a talent for languages. I knew what it was like to stand face-to-face with someone in a strange place and not be able to communicate even simple things. I wanted to help people understand each other. That was more important to me than anything else."

"So if I want to get out of Willow Valley, I should find the fastest way out. If that's a diploma, then that should be my goal."

"That's one way of looking at it. But you don't have to hate where you are while you're accomplishing your goal. Don't you think you can have some fun at the same time?"

He flipped off the baseball cap. "With Dad breathing down my neck?"

"Why do you think he does that?"

Travis ran the bill of the cap through his fingers. After some hesitation, he blurted out, "Because he feels responsible for me."

"I think it's more than that. He loves you."

"Like you said, you haven't known him very long."

"I get thrown into situations with people, and I'm pretty good at seeing what's below the surface. Your dad loves you and wants to protect you. He wants what's best for you. Do you ever try to talk about all this with him?"

Travis snapped his cap down on the sofa beside him. "He doesn't want to listen to what I have to say."

Forgetting she'd ever been thirsty, Meg sat forward in her chair and set her lemonade glass on the coffee table. "Travis, try to talk to him, tell him what you want, what you feel. It will help you both."

Travis shook his head. "It'll just stir up trouble. I know it."

She couldn't give up that easily, and she didn't want Travis to give up that easily. "Will you think about it?"

He shrugged. "Maybe." After a pause, he said, "You never really answered me about you and dad."

"I'm going back to Washington soon, Travis. So nothing can happen with me and your dad."

He didn't look quite satisfied with her answer. She wasn't satisfied herself, but she didn't know what else to tell him. Closing the topic for now, she asked, "Do you still want that cake?"

He looked at the stack of photographs on the table, then he looked back at her. "Sure. Chocolate's my favorite."

Meg went to the kitchen. She didn't mind talking about Travis's feelings, but she didn't want to analyze hers too closely. Cake and pictures would distract them both.

Since Travis had walked to Ned and Lily's, Meg asked if he'd like a ride home. He accepted, the conversation between them flowing smoothly about the places she'd been. She couldn't tell him about her work since much of it was classified, but she could tell him about the sights she'd seen.

He was enthralled.

When Meg pulled up in front of Logan's house, both the sheriff's car and the sedan were parked in the driveway. "It looks as if your dad's here now."

"Yeah. I wonder why. Unless he came home to check up on me."

Meg heard the anger in Travis's voice. Before they could get out of the car, Logan stepped out onto the porch and strode toward them. When Travis opened his door, Logan demanded, "Where were you? I called and you weren't here."

"Don't worry. If I take off again, I'll leave a note," Travis said sarcastically.

Logan rubbed his hand across his forehead. "Travis, it would help if you'd try to work with me on this."

"If you mean telling you minute by minute where I'll be, forget it. For four months, I took care of myself. I can do it now, too."

"You took such good care of yourself I had to pick you up at a hospital!"

Travis climbed out and slammed the door, then took off for the house without another look at Logan.

"Travis, I'm not finished talking to you...."

Travis ignored his father and went inside.

Logan came around to Meg's open window. "Where did you find him?"

"I didn't find him anywhere. He came to see me— to look at the photographs I mentioned. Logan, he's sixteen. He wants to be treated like an adult, not a child."

Anger creased Logan's brow and was evident in his words. "When he starts behaving like an adult, I'll treat him like one."

She remembered everything Travis had said, the sense that he wanted to get closer to his father but didn't know how. "You'll lose him if you keep this up."

Logan tightened his hands into fists, his body rigid. "I didn't ask for your advice."

"No, you didn't. But I'm telling you what I see. Like any boy Travis's age, he wants his father's approval. But for some reason, he doesn't think he can get it."

"You see Travis twice and you think you know him. I've spent sixteen years with him."

"Do *you* know him?" she asked softly.

Logan's face was etched with pain. "Thanks, Meg. I really need another guilt trip. He's wild and out of control, and nothing I say or do settles him down. He doesn't want to spend time with me. Can't you see that? Adults and their authority are taboo right now. Especially mine."

Meg had chosen a different route to rebel against her parents. She'd never felt she could earn their love. But instead of acting out to get their attention, she'd decided to go toward the love she knew she *could* get. She'd decided to live with Lily and Ned. And she'd thrown herself into her life's mission—helping people understand each other.

Travis was acting out. Something was definitely bothering him. For some reason, there was a wall between Logan and his son. Because of guilt, hurt, something else?

Silence fell between Meg and Logan, and distance grew though neither of them moved.

Logan finally said, his voice cold, "Maybe you should stay out of this."

Hurt stabbed deep, and she responded automatically, "Maybe I should." When she turned the key in the ignition, Logan stepped away from the car. He was granite-still, his expression hard. Nothing she could say would change his attitude; more than being angry with her, he was angry with himself because he couldn't find a solution. For that, he'd have to look into his heart.

Meg pulled away from the curb. Although she was tempted to look into her rearview mirror, she kept her gaze straight ahead. She was just a bystander. She didn't have a good reason to get involved. And she'd better remember that.

The next evening, Meg rocked Tomás on the front porch, a yearning in her heart as she did. He was so adorable with his black hair and beautiful dark eyes. He waved his arms, and she took one tiny fist in her hand. Already he'd grown.

She always felt excited when Carmen let her hold Tomás. Meg indulged herself a moment, fantasizing. A picture of Logan appeared in her mind. She tried to block out his face. She was thinking about mother-hood, not about him.

Tires on the gravel lane made her look up. Logan's car. Had she conjured him up? Sure, and she could make everything right between him and Travis, too, she thought wryly. She wished she could stop thinking about Logan and his son. No one could do anything about their relationship but them. If she knew what was good for her, she'd stay out of it. Logan had said as much.

She thought about hiding out in her room. She thought about leaving.

As Logan walked toward the front porch, he re-membered his last conversation with Meg. He'd caught a glimpse of her as he'd driven down the lane. Still, he wasn't prepared for her sitting on the swing like a beautiful madonna, holding Tomás in her arms. A need inside him, so basic it hurt, urged him closer to her while self-preservation shouted he should get back in his car and drive away as fast as he could.

But he wanted to say goodbye to Manuel and Carmen.

Meg looked up as he approached, her expression wary. No wonder. His attitude yesterday had been anything but pleasant. Not knowing where to start, he just said, "Lily invited me to supper."

"I see."

The invitation was obviously a surprise to Meg. It was also obvious that she was going to let him carry the ball. "She said Manuel and Carmen are leaving in the morning."

Meg looked at the baby, not at him. "Manuel feels he has to keep his commitment to his brother."

Logan nodded, feeling awkward at best, like a heel at the worst. "Doc has given them the okay to travel?"

"Yes, Carmen is getting her energy back, and the baby is gaining weight beautifully."

"And you're giving her a respite?"

Meg glanced up from the bundle in her arms. "Carmen wanted to help with supper, and I couldn't resist."

Couldn't resist. So unlike Shelley. Shelley had disliked all the aspects of taking care of an infant. She'd been much more comfortable as Travis had gotten older. Logan watched as Meg gently caressed the baby's cheek. So natural. The half smile on her lips hinted at her pleasure in simply holding the child.

Silence wrapped around them until Logan knew he had to bring what was bothering them both out into the open. "I'm sorry I took my frustration out on you yesterday."

"Frustration? It sounded more like anger. But you had a right. Your personal life is none of my business."

He'd expected her to just accept his apology and they'd go on from there. But not Meg. She was an all-or-nothing type of person. "I was angry at Travis."

She smoothed the baby's light blanket. "For visiting me?"

As soon as Meg's car had pulled away, he'd realized where the anger originated. "No. For scaring me again. All I could think about was him hitchhiking to God-knows-where."

Touching the front of her sandals to the porch floor, she swung slowly back and forth. "You're going to have to trust him."

"You've got to be kidding!"

"He feels your anger and your disapproval, and he's trying to get away from both."

"Look, I already know he ran away because of me...."

She stopped swinging and met his gaze squarely. "You don't know for sure why he ran away. Stop blaming yourself and look at the situation for what it is. He doesn't know how to get your attention, so he's doing it any way he can." Meg snapped her lips shut. Then she murmured, "I told myself I wasn't going to do that. You don't want me to be involved."

Logan climbed up the three wooden steps and sat beside her on the swing. "No, I didn't think I did. But it's obvious I'm not getting anywhere with Travis."

"He told me you made a deal with him."

Logan could smell baby powder and Meg's perfume. The combination was unsettling and damnably arousing. "You disapprove."

"I didn't say that."

"You don't have to."

"He has to motivate himself, Logan. He has to want a future as much as you want a future for him."

Just as Meg had caressed the baby's face, he couldn't keep himself from caressing hers. "You're a wise lady."

After a moment, she responded in a husky voice, "All those years I traveled with my parents, I felt as if there was some invisible wall between us. I tried to break it down. I tried being the best I could be. I studied hard. I tried to give them whatever they wanted. If they wanted me to be quiet, I occupied myself. If they wanted me to make friends in a new place, learn a new language, I did. Whatever they wanted. But I could never please them. At least, that's the way I saw it because I never felt their love."

Logan could see the hurt and sadness in Meg's eyes. He wanted to take her in his arms and erase all of it.

"Logan, I'm only telling you this so that you'll realize Travis might have some of those same feelings."

He pulled his hand away from her. "I didn't desert him or abandon him!"

"No, you didn't. And I know you love him. But he doesn't know that."

Logan stared straight ahead, into the fields and peace that had brought him here. "He can't quit school. Getting him a car will give him a reason to at least finish this year."

"What are you going to offer him his senior year?"

Logan couldn't get angry with Meg when she was only asking what he'd asked himself. "I'm hoping by then we'll straighten everything out."

Meg tilted her head and gave him a look that said she thought he was hoping for the impossible.

He rubbed the back of his neck. "Usually I'm a realist. But with Travis..." He shook his head. "Tell me something. I'd imagine you have to stay optimistic each time you go into a new situation. How do you do it? How do you keep past prejudices, past difficulties, from bogging you down?"

"How do you know I do?"

"Because you love what you do. You couldn't keep doing it if you didn't have hope that what you were doing would solve problems and help."

"I think you've gotten to know me a little too well."

Putting his finger under her chin, he turned her face toward his and realized exactly why he was here—despite logic and reason and timing. "I'd like to get to know you better."

Her eyes sparkled for a moment, and then he saw the sadness. "This isn't a good time for either of us."

"Time doesn't have anything to do with this."

"I'll be leaving after Thanksgiving."

"That's over two months away."

"Logan, I don't want to get hurt again."

"Again?"

She ducked her head and fidgeted with the baby's blanket. "It's not important."

"Everything about you is important."

Meg kept her head bowed, but Logan wasn't going to let her evade him this time. He had been angry yesterday...with himself, with Travis, with her. With her because her opinion of him counted, and he didn't want it to. But he respected her. And what she'd said yesterday had stung—a little too much. He'd thought about it last night. He'd thought about changing his tactics with Travis. He'd thought about Meg. And he knew he wanted to kiss her again. Now.

When he slipped his hand under her hair, she gazed up at him. He saw the same desire, the same need. He brushed her lips lightly, teasing them both. As his tongue slid between her lips, he heard her catch her breath. He was about to take advantage of her yielding when the screen door opened.

"Uh, supper's ready, you two. Unless you'd rather stay out here..."

Logan lifted his head and caught the sly smile on Lily's face. He felt like smiling himself—for the first time in a long time.

Logan watched from the barn door as Meg and Carmen strapped the infant seat into the truck. Manuel checked the oil as Ned looked on. The couple planned to leave in the early hours of the morning. He ducked into the barn to look for rope. Manuel could use it to tie down whatever they put in the bed of the truck. Lily, Ned and Meg had given the couple the cradle for the baby plus a few other things.

The late sun's rays danced through the open door, and the heat of the day lingered in the hay stacked along one wall. Logan found the rope coiled on a hook above buckets, a pitchfork and a broom. He heard footsteps but didn't turn.

"Did you find it?"

Aware of Meg the way he'd never been aware of another woman, Logan knew she was there before she spoke. During dinner, he'd caught her watching him as often as she'd caught him watching her. Her soft footsteps on the hay and old wood created an expectancy in him.

"Right over here."

She seemed to bring the sunlight inside with her. She definitely brought warmth. Her yellow T-shirt lay gently over her breasts, the material gathering at her slim waist. Her jeans weren't tight, but snug enough to hint at the curves underneath.

She stopped a foot from him and looked around the barn. "When I'm in D.C., I miss the smell of hay and barn timber. I miss the meadows and streams and woods to walk in. There's a peace here I haven't found anywhere else."

"That's why I wanted to move here. But I'm not going back. You are."

She stooped to the bales of hay and picked up a handful. "I fill up when I'm here. When I'm in D.C. or traveling, the work makes me forget about the necessity of time alone in the country."

"We haven't talked about Costa Rica."

"I told you...."

He took the hay from her hand and let it flutter to the floor. "I know what you told me. But whenever you talk about going back to work, I see fear and confusion in your eyes, not anticipation."

"I don't want to talk about it."

"Why?"

"Because...because already I feel some kind of connection with you."

A connection that was gaining strength any time they were together. "And you don't want to make it any stronger."

She shook her head.

"Because you were hurt once?" he asked gently.

"It's more complicated than that."

Her wide eyes spoke the messages he felt inside. Neither of them was putting them into words. "Then let's do something very simple. Something we both want."

Meg's warmth and light came with her as he drew her closer. She came willingly as if she knew he needed both unconditionally, with no restrictions.

He didn't even remember his arms surrounding her. But he knew the first moment his lips touched hers, everything in him came alive. When they'd returned from Richmond and he'd kissed her, he'd blamed the intensity on overreaction after an exhausting day. But this kiss had nothing to do with overreaction or fatigue. And there was nothing simple about it or the desire and needs that came with it.

Sex had ceased being a need for him. After Shelley's death, he'd found the energy necessary to find a satisfactory partner was better spent elsewhere. He'd denied physical needs before—often during his marriage. But now he couldn't deny yearnings that were more potent than any he'd ever experienced.

When Meg parted her lips, he took full advantage of her yielding, pulling her tighter against him and sweeping her mouth with his tongue. Her sweetness, her softness, made his heart pound. He longed for more—her delicate hands on his body, her satin skin against his, her heat surrounding him. Just the thought stoked the fire already primed to burn out of control.

He pulled her T-shirt out of her jeans, and she didn't protest. As his hand skimmed up her back, he felt her shiver of response. Her tongue danced with his until he knew she wanted him as much as he wanted her. He unhooked her bra, longing to touch more of her, longing to touch her intimately.

Her hands stroked the muscles of his back and restlessly moved to his backside. Logan felt ready to explode. He didn't need Meg's language skills to interpret what was happening between them. Their bodies cried out for each other, and they both understood. Meg's soft moans and his groan of excruciatingly sweet arousal didn't need any interpretation.

He slipped his hand between them, even though that meant unwanted space between their bodies. But their tongues continued to mate as if to make up for the deprivation. When his fingertips touched her breast, she made a noise in her throat, a sound of approval and encouragement. She was so soft, so responsive, so wonderfully a woman. His thumb found her nipple, and the feel of it gave him so much pleasure, he forgot to breathe.

But air didn't matter, and the shadows dimming the barn didn't matter; only he and Meg and the pleasure they could give each other mattered. When he took her nipple between his thumb and forefinger, she yanked his shirt from his jeans and nestled her fingers in the hair on his chest. Nothing had ever felt so right.

The slam of the tailgate of Manuel's truck shattered the fall of night, the momentum of their passion.

Meg went still, then abruptly pulled away as if everything about Logan burned her. She stumbled. Shaking himself loose from the haze of desire, he realized he didn't want her to regret any part of what had happened. He enfolded her in his arms and, even when she tried to pull away, he held tight.

But she wouldn't let him keep her there. She stepped away, murmuring, "Someone might come in."

He didn't argue with her. "Meg, don't be embarrassed."

She hooked her bra and, as best she could, tucked her T-shirt in her jeans. "I'm not embarrassed, I'm sorry. We'll only get hurt, Logan. You know it and I know it."

All he knew was that *not* kissing her, touching her and talking to her hurt. "So you can just dismiss whatever's happening?"

"No, of course I can't. But I should know better than to let it go too far."

"It's already gone too far."

Her gaze met his. "What do you want, Logan?"

"You."

She blushed. "Sex."

"For a talented interpreter, you've got that wrong. And I think you know it." He tucked his shirt into his jeans. "You think about it, Meg. And you ask yourself the question if all *you* wanted just then was sex." Angry because she wasn't facing up to what was happening between them, he took the rope from the hook on the wall and headed for the door. If he stayed, he'd take her in his arms again.

Until she was sure that was what she wanted, too, he'd have to keep his distance. Or one of them *would* get hurt.

Chapter Six

Gibson's Grocery had stood on the corner of Main and First Avenue ever since Meg could remember. It had seen few changes. Green siding now covered the weatherboard for maintenance reasons, and the refrigerated cases in the back of the grocery had been modernized. Olan Gibson had lengthened his store hours to nine in the evening, as well as afternoons on Sundays, and his brown hair had thinned, turning salt-and-pepper. But the twinkle in his eyes and the quirk of his smile remained the same, constants in a changing world.

Lily needed a few groceries and preferred shopping at Gibson's rather than at the sparkling but sterile supermarket in the strip shopping center on the west end of town, where new housing developments had overtaken the landscape for the past five years. Meg stood beside her aunt as she reached into the produce case for a head of lettuce.

Meg picked up a bag of carrots and, when she put them in the cart, she noticed the pallor on her aunt's face. "Aunt Lily, what's wrong?"

"Nothing, dear. Just some indigestion."

"You had indigestion earlier this week. Maybe you should call Doc Jacobs."

"I'll think about it. I wonder where Ned disappeared to. He said something about the hardware store but...speak of the devil." Lily nodded to the door. "Look who he has with him."

Ned clapped Logan on the back and said to the women, "This man said he was coming in for a fresh turkey sub. I thought maybe we could all get one and go over to the park. We can pick up the groceries later."

Lily and Ned exchanged a look that told Meg better than words that the two were matchmaking. She even wondered if this little trip had been planned. She couldn't think about Logan, definitely not look at him, without remembering their last kiss. When he'd left the barn, she'd composed herself as best she could and gone outside. Not long afterward, Logan had shaken Manuel's hand, said goodbye to Carmen and the baby and left...without another look at her, without another word just for her.

"Yes, why don't we do that?" Lily agreed, and went to the deli case. "Four turkey subs, Olan," she said to the grocer behind the case. And four of those bottles of juice."

Neither Meg nor Logan protested. Logan's gaze met hers as he held the door for her. She felt the fire from the kiss all over again.

With school back in session, only a few people strolled through the park. No one else sat at the weatherworn picnic tables sequestered under a canopy of maples and elms. Lily acted as hostess, spreading napkins for place mats. She and Ned kept up a constant run of conversation as the four of them ate, though Meg did notice that her aunt barely touched her sandwich. Logan commented on the warm weather and the chances of the high-school football team this season. Meg contributed what she knew about Manuel and Carmen's departure, confirming that the couple had promised to stop back in Willow Valley when they drove through to Florida. She didn't admit how much she missed them, how much she missed rocking Tomás in her arms.

She couldn't finish her sub. She wasn't hungry to begin with. Logan didn't have any trouble with his. But after he'd finished, he said, "I have to get back to the office."

Lily and Ned exchanged another one of those looks. "Stay a few more minutes until Meg finishes and keep her company. Ned and I will go get the groceries."

And before either Logan or Meg could comment, the older couple walked away from them.

"They're not very subtle," Meg said with a grimace.

"I thought about calling you," Logan informed her with his usual honesty. But his frown told her he'd thought better of it.

"I've been thinking about you, too," she admitted. Between worrying about Logan and going back to D.C., she hadn't thought of much else.

"But not enough to call."

"I didn't know what to say." She felt her cheeks grow hot, remembering the barn, remembering her response to him.

"So you think if you ignore me I'll go away? Just as your fears of going back to work will go away?"

His words stabbed her, but when her gaze confronted his, she knew he didn't intend to be mean. His expression softened, and he came around to her side of the table. Instead of sitting beside her, he sat on the table, his long legs propped on the bench. "Talk to me, Meg."

"I thought you had to go back to work."

He brushed his hand along her cheek, then slowly ran his thumb along her bottom lip. She closed her eyes and willed the trembling to stop.

"Is that what you want?"

The timbre of his voice urged her to open her eyes and look at him. "No. But I'm not sure I can trust my decisions right now."

"What are you doubting? What's bothering you?"

"I am afraid to go back to my job. I'm afraid I'll make another mistake."

"What mistake did you make?"

"It's my fault the terrorist went off the deep end and started shooting. It's my fault. I said the wrong thing. What if I do it again?"

"Meg..."

"It could happen. Anything could happen. What if I freeze? What if the words won't come? What if I'm the only one who can speak the language, and the full responsibility of everyone's safety rests on me?"

"You'll do your best."

"And what if my best isn't good enough? What if instead of me getting hurt, someone loses their life?"

"You can't live your life in fear of making a mistake!"

Anger bubbled up. "That's logical and easy to say, but I can't feel that way." Logan's leg brushed her arm, and the anger faded away. Is this how he'd felt when she'd offered him advice?

"So what are you going to do?"

She shook her head. "I don't know. I'm supposed to go to D.C. to a fund-raiser in a few weeks. Maybe once I'm back there, I'll feel differently."

"And what about us?"

She frowned. "We're almost as complicated."

He chucked her gently under the chin. "Oh, you think so? Is being friends so complicated?"

His large body next to her, his scent all around her, his face leaning toward hers with its character and determination and kindness, made her ask bemusedly, "Friends?" Suddenly the reality of their kiss and the definition of the word clashed. Leaning just a tad away, she tried to tease, "Friends who kiss?"

He held her chin in his palm, and the heat from his hand traveled through her whole body. "Friends who kiss and learn about each other and let whatever happens happen."

She withdrew from his touch, protecting herself. "I don't live like that."

"You don't have friends?"

"I don't jump without a parachute."

"What kind of a man do you think I am, Meg?"

"I don't know. I don't know if you go to bars on weekends and pick up women. I don't know if sex means more to you than the moment."

"Don't you?"

She was building walls, maybe trying to shock him into going away. She was scared to death to get close to him—scared because of the last time she'd fallen in love, scared because she didn't live in Willow Valley and he did.

"I'm not ready to jump into anything, either," he said. "Lord knows, I've got enough to handle right now with Travis. But I like being around you. And I *really* like kissing you." His eyes twinkled as his crooked smile melted her.

She returned his smile. "I think you've had a lot of training in learning how to convince and charm."

"You think I'm charming?"

His smile was so sexy, his expression so ingenuous, she laughed.

He cradled her head and drew her toward him. His kiss was easy, no demands, no promises. But there was excitement and a sense of adventure that left her breathless.

Logan pulled away. "I'll walk you to Gibson's."

She felt as if she were traveling to a foreign country, one where she'd never been before. When she looked up at Logan, she didn't see the uncertainty she felt, and she wondered just how well she knew him.

Michael Holden closed the folder on his desk. "It sounds good, Meg. The letters to the parents went out last week. Parents aren't as involved with teenagers as they are with elementary-aged children, so you might only get four or five per class. And these days, with both parents working, it's tough for them to *be* involved."

"I'm hoping the students will get a peek of other cultures and widen their perspective."

"Well, something you said sparked Travis Mac-Donald. He was always a good student without much effort. Now he's putting forth some effort. He's interested in the student-exchange program."

"I'm glad he's looking into it. You know, I could use some help with the technical aspects of the presentation on Friday, setting up the slide projector and that type of thing. Do you think he'd be interested?"

Michael checked the schedule of classes on the board on the wall. "He's at lunch. Why don't you go to the cafeteria and ask him? He usually sits with his friends at the table nearest the back exit."

"I think I'll do that."

"You're trying to get him more involved, aren't you?"

"He needs roots, something to hold on to."

"Can I ask you something personal?"

She cocked her head.

"Are you and Logan seeing each other?"

And how was she supposed to answer that? She hadn't heard from Logan since he'd walked her to Gibson's a few days ago. "Not formally."

He studied her for a moment. "If some night you decide you'd like to go to dinner, give me a call."

Michael Holden was a nice man and very good-looking to boot. But she didn't feel the pull toward him she felt toward Logan.

He must have seen her answer on her face. "Think about it."

She smiled. "I will."

After Meg left Michael's office, she headed for the cafeteria. She entered the large, noisy room, remembering lunches in high school, the rowdiness, the chattering, the food fights that occasionally broke out as teenagers let off steam. The boys at Travis's table shoveled in food and talked around their forks.

One of them whistled as Meg walked toward the table. Her navy slacks and oxford shirt were nothing to snag attention. She ignored the blonde with the leering smile and addressed Travis. "Can I talk to you for a few minutes?"

"Woo-eee, Travis. Who's the babe?" the blonde asked, his elbow jabbing Travis.

Travis scrambled from the bench. "Stuff it, Kyle." He walked with Meg over to the corner of the room. Digging his hands into his pockets, he asked, "Is there a problem?"

"No. Not at all. I wondered if you'd like to help me set up the equipment for my presentation on Friday."

"What equipment?"

"The slide projector mainly. I have enough to keep my mind on without worrying about the order of slides and running the projector. Would you like to help?"

Travis glanced over at the table where his friends sat.

"If you don't want to, Mr. Holden can get someone else. I understand if you're worried about what your friends might think."

"I don't care what they think. Besides...since I took off and managed to come back alive, they think I'm cool."

She smiled. "You *are* cool but not because you ran away and survived."

"Oh, yeah. Real cool."

"Don't sell yourself short, Travis."

He shifted on his sneakers, uncomfortable with her praise. "I'll help you."

"Can you come in early? I'm going to set up in study hall C."

"What time?"

"Is eight o'clock too early?"

"Nope."

"How are you and your dad getting along?"

"We're not."

Meg decided maybe what these two males needed was a referee. But she wasn't sure if she wanted to volunteer for the job.

Friday evening, Lily handed Meg a stack of dishes to load into the dishwasher. "Word has it your presentation at the high school went very well."

Meg shook her head and smiled. "Word" had probably been spread by one parent who had talked to so-and-so, who had talked to so-and-so. "The kids seemed to enjoy it. At first they thought I was going to lecture and they could sleep. But when I made it clear I wanted their comments and questions, they weren't shy."

"How'd it go with Travis?"

Meg had told her aunt she'd asked him to assist her. "He was a big help. I think his reputation went up a notch because the other students thought he 'knew' me."

"You counted on that, didn't you?"

"I'd hoped. Now, if I'd have bombed, I don't know what would have happened to Travis's reputation."

The only discordant note had been the tension between Travis and Logan. Travis had ignored his father from the moment Logan had entered the study hall, and he'd pretended to be too busy to talk afterward. Logan had simply nodded to Meg and left after the period was over.

A warm breeze fluttered the leaves of the philodendron sitting on the kitchen window's ledge. Meg looked up and saw her uncle attempting to climb onto the garage roof. "Oh, my gosh."

"What's the matter? Did you— Ned! Good Lord. He's going to break his neck."

Meg hurried out the back door, her aunt close behind her.

When they reached the garage, Meg took hold of the ladder to steady it. "Uncle Ned, this really isn't a good idea."

"Ned, you get down here this instant. You're too old to be up there," Lily called.

"'Old' has nothing to do with it. I need to fix the shingles before winter. If I don't do it, I'll have to pay someone to do it. That's foolish."

"What's foolish is you being up on that ladder," Lily argued. "You should have had Manuel do it."

"I didn't realize how bad it was until after he left."

"What am I going to do if you break your neck?" Lily asked.

"I'm not going to break my neck." The ladder wobbled as Ned found his footing on the roof. "Stop distracting me, and I'll be just fine."

"Ned, I think these women are worried about you. Maybe we could work out another deal."

Still gripping the ladder, Meg glanced over her shoulder, though she'd know that deep baritone anywhere.

Lily edged closer to Logan and murmured, "You get him down from there, and I'll bake you apple dumplings every week for a month."

Logan chuckled. "Now, that's a bribe I can't refuse."

His gaze found Meg's. There was no laughter in his eyes, but a depth and intensity that took her breath away. She gripped the ladder harder.

Logan called to her uncle, "You told me you'd show me how to refinish that old chest I bought. What if I nail on the shingles in repayment?"

"Some of the wood might be rotted."

"You buy the plywood, I'll make the repairs."

"Did these women call you before they came running out here?" Ned asked with a ferocious scowl.

"We most certainly did not," Lily protested.

Ned rubbed his hand over his forehead and peered down at Logan. "All right. Seems as though these two will have a conniption if I don't agree. But I'll help you sand that chest, too. I'm not going to just stand by and watch. And I supervise the roof."

Logan crossed to Meg. His hand brushed hers as he said, "I'll hold it for him."

She stepped aside, her hand tingling, her whole being vibrating because Logan was so close.

"Sounds good to me, Ned," Logan agreed.

"Now come down," Lily demanded.

Ned turned around and found the first step on the ladder. As he descended, he grumbled, "If it was up to you, I'd sit on the porch rocking all day. That's no life."

Logan waited until the older man was safely on the ground before he moved away.

Ned wagged his finger at his wife. "Now, don't you scold. I was perfectly safe. These legs are as sturdy as ever."

"But your balance isn't."

"Lily, you worry too much."

Logan cleared his throat. "Do you mind if I go up and see what we need?"

"Offhand, I'd say two boxes of shingles. See what you think."

"I'll hold the ladder," Meg said.

Logan didn't argue with her but started climbing up. Ned put his arm around his wife's shoulders. "Come on, darlin'. They don't need us watching."

As her aunt and uncle walked back to the house, Meg watched Logan climb the ladder. His jeans pulled snug with each step. She smiled at the great view. As if he'd read her thoughts, he glanced at her over his shoulder. Caught looking, she felt a flush creep up her cheeks.

"I could hold the ladder while you climb up," he teased, eyeing her tan twill slacks and red blouse.

"No, thanks. Roofs aren't my specialty."

After a smile that made her want to follow him up the ladder, he climbed to the top and stood on the slightly slanted roof. He walked from side to side, bending to examine the shingles. Surefooted and balanced, he looked as comfortable on the roof as he did on the ground, and Meg couldn't take her eyes from him.

His shoulders were broad against the blue sky. His hands, as he ran them over the shingles, were deft and sure. He liked to touch. She could tell. The sensation of his hand on her face lasted long after the moment. Was that because of him? Or her?

It didn't much matter. His touch made her want more of it. No man had ever caused that reaction in her. She'd gone through life believing she didn't need a close relationship with a man. And after her experience with Todd, she'd been sure of it. Was she simply afraid? Was she afraid she couldn't please a man any more than she could please her parents? Was she afraid of an abandonment that would hurt even worse than her parents leaving her in Willow Valley?

Why hadn't she asked herself these questions before? The answer to that came swiftly. Because Logan was different than other men she'd met. The way she felt around him was different. His effect on her was different. Maybe because when they'd delivered Manuel and Carmen's baby, her barriers had been down. Logan knew how to face life honestly. Had his no-games attitude reached a place inside of her that was tired of surface conversation, diplomacy and politeness?

The questions rang in her head with no definite answers.

Suddenly Logan beckoned to her. "Come on up and sit on the edge with me. The view is great."

"You *are* kidding."

He smiled. "C'mon. I'll make sure you don't fall off. I'll even steady the ladder."

An adventurous imp inside her—which didn't mind airplanes but wasn't too crazy about walking across bridges—pushed her to go to the foot of the ladder. When she put her foot on the first rung, she thought she might be crazy. But when she looked up at Logan and saw the twinkle in his eyes, she didn't care. She wanted to sit up there beside him.

When she climbed to the top, he took her hand and didn't let go until she sat on the roof. The landscape spread before them like a peaceful pastoral painting, rich in color and texture and mood. The day's sun spread its rays across the sky, leaving streaks of orange and brilliant pink. Lavender led into blue as heaven and earth met at the horizon.

Logan took in a deep breath. His thigh brushed hers, and she felt as if they were alone in a different world.

"Sitting up here, I wonder how problems get so big." His voice was deep and husky and washed over Meg, filling her with his sadness.

"Maybe you and Travis should come up here and sit on the roof."

His gaze caught hers. "I was thinking about you and what you do."

"Were you?"

"I think Travis and I have come to a stalemate."

"Only if neither of you tries to move again."

"He doesn't want me around, Meg. He picks an argument every time we're together, as if he wants to drive me further away. I came to your presentation at school so he'd see I care about him. He made it clear he didn't want me there."

"It would help if you could see his point of view."

"Do you think I haven't tried?"

"I don't know."

Logan's jaw tensed, and his expression grew hard. "Well, I do know."

Meg had to say something she knew might make Logan angry, might make him less eager to be around her or talk with her. But she felt it needed to be said. "I think something is holding you away from Travis."

Logan was silent. And there was an anger in the silence that shook Meg's heart and the peace of the countryside.

In a fluid motion, Logan stood. He climbed onto the ladder and pinned her with a look that said she'd gone too far. "I'll hold the ladder for you as you come down."

"Logan..."

"Enough, Meg."

The words were terse, and Meg had the distinct feeling Logan wanted to say more but was refraining. Maybe that was the problem. He refrained too much. Maybe if he got it all out... But as he made his way to the ground, she didn't know if she dare suggest it. She didn't want to sever their bond of friendship, if she hadn't already. She should have kept quiet. She should have minded her own business. She shouldn't care as much as she already did.

She'd expected Logan to be striding away when she neared the last rung. But he continued to hold the ladder. His face was hard, etched with the anger she'd heard in his voice and sensed with her heart. If she didn't care, she could leave more unsaid.

She didn't know if she was pleading for herself as a young girl or Travis when she said, "He needs you, Logan. Don't turn your back on him. Show him you love him. Show him his words and actions hurt you. Don't just stoically accept—"

Logan's eyes darkened as he reached for her. She never thought to be afraid...not of Logan. When his mouth crushed hers, she fleetingly wondered if this was his way of shutting her up. It certainly was effective. Rational thought fled as his tongue parted her lips and thrust inside. The thrusts were rhythmic and deliberately arousing, and she could envision them mating in the same primal way. Logan was rigid and hard as he pressed against her. Was he trying to shock her?

She tore away, more affected than she wanted to admit. Holding on to the ladder instead of Logan, she almost felt hurt, almost felt... "You can't use me to soothe feelings you don't want to talk about. You can't use me to—"

"I wasn't using you for anything," he snapped. "I was trying to show you nothing is as simple as it seems. Not between me and Travis and not between me and you. Don't you get it yet, Meg? You can't fix everything with a few right words."

"No, you can't. You need to explore the feelings behind the words. Why can't you talk to Travis? Why can't you reach out to him? Why...?"

"Stop it, Meg. Don't you see that I don't have the answers? Solutions aren't as easy as adding a column of numbers."

"Have you honestly looked for the solution?"

A crow cawed. The quiet, which before had been restful, was now abrasive. Logan broke it. "If you have to ask that, then we really don't know each other at all, and maybe that kiss and the passion behind it is all that will ever be between us. I don't think this conversation is about me and Travis at all. I think it's your way of pushing me away, making me too uncomfortable to want to stay around. You don't have to push me away, Meg. If you don't want me here, all you have to do is say it."

She couldn't tell him to go, yet she couldn't ask him to stay. He was right. Nothing was simple anymore. "I don't know what to say."

"Neither do I, so maybe we'd better leave it at that. Tell Ned I'll be over tomorrow morning to work on the roof."

As Logan waited, she wanted to ask him to think about what she'd said and tell him she'd think about what he'd said. But she couldn't, and maybe that was another way of pushing him away.

Logan just arched his brows and cocked his head expectantly.

All she could manage was "I'll tell him to expect you."

Logan frowned and nodded, then walked to his car. Right before he opened his door, he gazed at her again.

Meg felt as if he could see right through her. She turned and walked to the house. Dealing with Logan had become as dangerous as being kidnapped by a terrorist. She had to figure out why.

Chapter Seven

The stones crunched under Meg's feet as she jogged back to the house. Breathing fast but feeling better than she had after tossing and turning all night, she slowed her jog to a walk, absorbing the sunshine, letting the heat beat through her, trying to forget about her confrontation with Logan last night. Jogging always gave her a sense of well-being—muscles working, blood flowing, adrenaline rushing. Logan's face appeared unbidden in front of her eyes. Yep, the adrenaline rushing. She remembered too well the thrill of it when Logan had kissed her...and touched her....

Lily had heard her roaming in the middle of the night when she'd finally gone to the kitchen for some milk, hoping it would make her sleepy. Her aunt had asked what was wrong. Meg had simply said, "I have too much time on my hands during the day, so I'm not sleepy at night."

Lily hadn't bought it. She'd smiled and said, "Maybe you have too much time on your hands at night."

Meg's shock must have shown.

Her aunt's smile had spread into a grin, and she'd said gently, "I always sleep better when your uncle is holding me." Then she'd disappeared down the hall without another word.

Meg did long for someone to hold her. Not just someone—Logan. She wished she could get the man off her mind. She wished she could forget his words. *You don't have to push me away, Meg. If you don't want me here, all you have to do is say it.*

She pushed away so she wouldn't get hurt. It wasn't his conclusion that had kept her awake most of the night; the truth of it had nudged her until it echoed too loudly to drown out.

Though Meg tried to rush inside and hurry up the stairs before Lily could continue their middle-of-the-night conversation, she only managed three steps when her aunt's voice stopped her. "You had a phone call. Some office in Lynchburg. I put the number by the phone in the kitchen. The woman said she'd be there until noon."

Meg glanced at the clock on the mantel. Ten. Logan would probably be here soon, and she'd rather not be anywhere around…at least not until she figured out a few things. But the call shouldn't take long.

Lily stood at the sink, coring apples as Meg made the call.

A receptionist answered and put Meg through to Victoria Lee.

"Ms. Lee, this is Meg Dawson returning your call."

"Miss Dawson, it is a pleasure to speak with you."

Meg guessed the cultured voice testified to more than one language in the woman's upbringing. "I'm sorry I don't recognize your name. Have we met?"

"No, we have not. A friend of mine sent me the article that appeared in the *Willow Valley Courier.* I made some calls and discovered you were taking time off and living in Willow Valley. I have a position I'd like you to consider. I run the Lee adoption service here in Lynchburg. We are an international adoption agency and are looking for a liaison who is fluent in many languages and could communicate with the officials and personnel in the countries we deal with as well as with the couples who want to adopt."

"You're offering me a job?"

"I understand this is quite different from the work you are used to. But I'd like to set up an interview with you if possible so we can discuss it. Please give me the time to show you the value in the work we do. Would that be agreeable to you?"

The offer took Meg completely by surprise. "Can you give me some time to think about it?"

"I'd rather give you the time *after* you give me the opportunity to present my offer. We will need to fill the position by February and have started our search early to find someone with the qualifications we desire. Can you come in Wednesday morning so we can discuss it?"

Meg had to smile at Victoria Lee's persistence. "All right, I can come in on Wednesday. What's your address?"

After Meg wrote down the address of the agency and directions and ended the call, Lily studied her and asked, "Something to keep you busy?"

Meg told her aunt about Victoria Lee's job offer.

"What do you think?" Lily asked.

"I don't know. I've always loved my work."

"But something's keeping you from it."

Lily's perception shouldn't surprise Meg, but it did...often. "I've needed time to rest, to think."

"What's there to think about, honey? Unless you're thinking about not going back."

"Aunt Lily..."

Lily placed the apples on the cutting board, lined up in a row. "Would that be so terrible? Changing your mind about what you want to do?"

A loud meowing answered Lily before Meg could. Automatically Meg went to the screen door, opened it and picked up Leo. She cuddled the kitten in the crook of her arm. "It's not that simple. I have a life in Washington, an excellent reputation. I get paid well and I'm self-sufficient. I don't have to depend on anyone."

Lily dried her hands on a towel and pulled the flour canister toward her. "And why do you think changing your job would bother all that?"

Meg rubbed Leo's neck and heard him purr. "Maybe it wouldn't."

"Honey, there's nothing wrong with depending on someone. I know you're afraid to, I know Iris and Joe let you down over and over again. But that doesn't mean everyone will."

Meg went still. "This has nothing to do with Mother and Dad."

Her aunt faced her, concern and compassion in her eyes. "I think it does. But that's something *you* have to think about."

Leo rubbed against Meg's hand. Reflexively, she cuddled and stroked him. "I'm going upstairs to change. And then I'm driving into town."

"Logan's coming."

"I know."

Lily didn't say a word, but Meg knew her aunt was thinking plenty. One tough decision at a time was enough.

"I really should get to work on the roof," Logan said as Lily set the apple dumpling in front of him.

"You need some nourishment before you start. You said you didn't have anything but coffee for breakfast."

He smiled at the woman who was so good at taking care of everyone. "That's the usual."

She shook her head. "You and Meg."

"Where is she?"

"Upstairs, taking a shower. She got an interesting call this morning. Some adoption agency offered her a job in Lynchburg."

He couldn't keep the question inside. "What did she say?"

"She's meeting with the woman on Wednesday."

Hope warming his heart, he dug into the apple dumpling. He shouldn't care what Meg decided. She was obviously running from more than him.

A few minutes later, Meg came hurrying into the kitchen, a kitten nestled in the crook of her arm. "Aunt Lily, I'm going to duck out now before..."

"Before I get here?" Logan asked, raising his head. His body responded to her appearance in coral cuffed shorts and a rib-knit T-shirt with a lace-up neckline. What he would like to do to that ribbon... If he knew what was good for him, he'd let her duck out and he'd get the roof started without distraction.

Lily interrupted the tense silence. "I have laundry to gather." With a knowing look at both of them, she headed for the stairs.

Meg's reluctance to be around Logan irritated him. "I told you before, if you want me to leave, all you have to do is say so."

Avoiding his gaze, she sat down in a chair across from him, the kitten on her lap. "I like you, Logan."

He leaned forward. "Then stop running away from me."

"I'm not running away from you any more than you're running away from Travis."

Anger erupted again, and he checked it. "Honest to God, Meg, don't you ever let up?"

"If we can't even talk about it..."

He pushed back his chair and stood. "Maybe that's the problem. You want to talk. I want to do something else." He couldn't keep the edge from his voice, or the tension of unfulfilled desire. "When you're ready to talk about that or, better yet, do something about it, I'll be on the roof."

The surprise on her face told him his bluntness had probably just ruined any chance he had. But his dreams were getting more vivid, his response to her more intense, every time he saw her. Maybe bluntness was what they both needed.

He left her sitting there, the kitten in her lap, her brown eyes wide and confused. He pulled in a deep breath and went into the backyard, looking forward to ripping off shingles.

* * *

Sweat dripped from Logan's brow as he straightened and stood on the garage roof. Impatiently he swiped the perspiration with his wristband. The sun beat down on him from its high-noon position. He needed something to drink. He also needed to have his head examined. If Meg had been skittish around him before, now she'd probably ignore him completely.

It had been years since he'd wanted a woman the way he wanted her. In fact, he couldn't ever remember a woman affecting him the way Meg did. He crossed to the ladder and climbed down. He needed a break from the sun and his thoughts. If he remembered correctly, a stream ran through Ned's property. Without bothering to grab his shirt, Logan headed toward the water.

As soon as he stepped into the tree line, he heard the slight breeze ruffling the leaves, the whistles of chickadees and the ripple of water over rocks. All he could think about was splashing his face in the cool water and letting the peace surround him.

The peace vanished when he stepped closer to the stream and saw Meg. Oblivious to everything around her, she waded on a large rock in the middle of the stream, dangling her hand in the water. He walked toward her because he couldn't walk away. Standing at the bank, he called her name.

She gazed up at him. Only about ten feet separated them, but he felt it was more like the width of the world. She gingerly stepped from rock to rock until she found her footing on the bank. "I come down here to think."

He asked what was foremost on his mind, guessing it was foremost on hers. "Lily told me about your job offer. Are you considering staying here?"

She shook her head. "I can't."

"Why?"

"Because I wouldn't respect myself. I can't stay in Willow Valley because I'm afraid to go back."

"It's a damn good reason *not* to go back."

"I don't live my life that way. Just because I ignore a problem doesn't mean it will go away. I have to confront it to settle it."

Logan couldn't resist the vulnerability on her face, the honest way she faced life. He caressed her cheek, admiring Meg's strength and determination. Yet he wasn't sure either would bring her happiness. "Maybe we have to confront what's going on between us to settle it."

"We've done that."

Her breaths came faster, and he stroked her face again. "No, we haven't. We're resisting, pushing each other away so the sparks between us don't blaze out of control. Maybe we shouldn't be so afraid of the fire."

"Logan..."

He slipped his arm around her and bent closer. "Kiss me, Meg. As if you aren't afraid."

He thought she might back away. He thought what he'd said in the kitchen might make her angry. But she didn't look angry now. She looked as if she wanted to feel the fire as much as he did. His lips found hers, and the fire was the only thing that mattered.

Red-hot flames licked at him. As his tongue parted her lips, want and need rushed through him with such force and speed, he was hard and aching for satisfaction instantaneously. He'd always known runaway passion was dangerous. He'd never realized it would be so all consuming. Did Meg feel any of it? Could she deny it? Could she run from it?

Logan enclosed her tighter against him. She didn't protest; rather, she pressed her breasts against his chest and moaned in approval. He lifted her knit top and spread his fingers across her midriff. Her skin fascinated him. The satin softness of it. Everything about Meg fascinated him—her intelligence, her warmth, her genuine loveliness. He plunged his tongue deeper into her mouth—needing, searching, burning as he'd never burned before.

Meg had never played with fire. Caution had always guided most of her decisions. She collected information until her mind and heart united in deciding the best course for her. But now...here...caution floated away with the whistles of the chickadees. Logan's skin was hot, his chest hard, his scent intoxicating. And his touch created a longing inside her she couldn't begin to understand.

He pulled away and, when she protested, he came back to her again. His initial hunger transformed into teasing play, stoking her desire, making the longing become a living entity. He nibbled her bottom lip. She wanted more. He touched her bottom lip with his tongue. She wanted more. He slid his hands along the sides of her breasts, and she wanted so much more she couldn't comprehend the need.

Frustrated by her own need, not knowing what she wanted most—whether she wanted to touch him, or if she wanted him to touch her—she slid her hands up his chest, reveling in the texture of his skin, the curling hair between her fingers, the sheer masculine power of

Logan. He groaned, and she kneaded his shoulders, loving the feel of him.

The tip of his tongue stroked against hers, then retreated. She chased him and found satisfaction in the deeper kiss. Logan knew what he was doing.

But did she?

She couldn't let fear keep her from living. But she couldn't let it keep her from working, either. If she didn't go back to her career, she'd feel like a quitter. She'd feel as if she failed. All her life, she'd felt as if she'd failed some test in her parents' eyes. She couldn't fail herself. She had to think about her future.

And Logan? She wanted to make love with him. The need was more than physical. But their situation was complicated enough.

And they were making it worse. She was making it worse by responding as if she was falling in love with him. Love. *No. She couldn't.*

She braced her hands on his chest and pushed away. His skin burned her, and she stuffed her hands in the pockets of her shorts to keep them safe . . . to keep her safe. Desire rippled through her until she almost lost her balance. But she spread her feet apart and closed her eyes, hoping the need would diminish, praying she was wrong about falling in love.

"Meg. Look at me." The authority in his voice vied with the huskiness of unfulfilled desire.

With a deep breath, she opened her eyes.

"What stopped you? What made the fear come back?"

"You. Me. What I have to do."

"You mean leaving Willow Valley."

"I mean going back to work."

He shook his head. "What drives you, Meg?" His gaze probed deep into her heart.

She reached inside for the reason she always confronted her fears. "It's not easy for a child to go to strange places, meet strange people and learn strange customs. But I did it over and over again. When I did, fear eventually subsided."

"Did your parents know you were afraid?"

"I hid it. I was afraid if they saw it, they wouldn't let me go with them."

"But you liked staying with Lily and Ned."

"Yes, but, Logan, they weren't my parents. I wanted to be with my parents. I wanted to make them proud."

His dark brows drew together. "So why did you choose to stay with Lily and Ned when you were older?"

Her voice softened. "Because by then, I knew Lily and Ned loved me. I'd figured out I could never earn my parents' love. I didn't stay because I was afraid to go. I stayed because I wanted to."

"So, if you're afraid of something, you feel you have to do it not to be afraid anymore?"

She nodded. "Yes."

He stood silent as the water rippled over the rocks and the leaves swished and the sun rose higher. "Are you afraid to make love with me?"

He'd caught her in a philosophical trap and he knew it. "That's not the same."

He grimaced. "Somehow I knew you'd say that." Walking to the edge of the bank, he gazed into the water.

Meg took a few more deep breaths wondering what would come next...wondering what *could* come next.

"I've been thinking about what you said ... about something holding me back from Travis."

She approached him slowly.

"If it weren't for Travis, Shelley and I might never have gotten married." He stuffed his hands in his jeans as the water rippled and rays of sun danced like diamonds on the water. "We weren't right for each other. She hated me being a cop. When she got pregnant, she didn't want to get married. But I convinced her it was best. This was our child. I couldn't contemplate not bringing him into the world or giving him away. So I only saw one solution."

"What happened after Travis was born?"

"She resented me. The demands of an infant, a child. She was lenient with Travis. As he grew older, I had to counteract that. I believed he should have chores and be accountable for them—that kind of thing. We moved to Willow Valley because I thought it would help. I wouldn't be a 'cop' per se. Life would be slower paced." He shook his head. "I should have realized we'd never want the same things. But hindsight is always twenty-twenty."

Meg suspected there was more Logan wasn't telling her. "You've always loved your son."

He turned from the stream then and looked at her, the memories clouding his eyes. "Yes. But there was this tension between Shelley and me that seemed to grow each day. I didn't understand it until the night she died."

"What was it?"

The lines on his face deepened, and the muscle in his jaw worked. "It doesn't matter anymore. What matters is that Travis always saw me as the bad guy. I enforced discipline and rules. I made him take out the garbage. And too many nights, I wasn't there to be part of putting him to bed, taking him roller-skating, reading to him. I thought moving to Willow Valley would change that. But he was twelve by then."

"Travis is a good kid, Logan."

"Maybe he is. But I'm not like you, Meg. I don't know how to nurture. Watching you with Manuel and Carmen's baby made me wonder how I ever thought I could be a good parent."

She took a step closer to him. How she wanted to ease his pain. How she wanted to help him find a bond with his son. "You're being too hard on yourself."

"No, I'm being realistic."

"It's never too late to learn or fix or start again. Not if two people are willing."

"But Travis isn't willing."

"Logan . . ."

"I don't want to argue with you," he said evenly.

"What do you want?" As soon as the question came out, she regretted it because she remembered their conversation in the kitchen.

Desire flashed in his eyes. Reaching out, he tenderly stroked her chin. "You know what I want."

"Satisfying some physical need won't solve anything."

"No, but we'd have a hell of a good time doing it."

The blush crawled up her cheeks, but she didn't take her gaze from him. She couldn't deny the strength of the attraction between them. But she could keep a lid on hers, for both their sakes.

When she didn't respond to his comment, he asked, "Are you going back to the house?"

"In a little while."

"More wading?"

"It's peaceful here."

He nodded as if he understood.

About an hour later, Meg called to Logan from the back door. "Lunch."

He waved at her from the roof so she'd know he heard. She didn't go inside right away, but watched him from the doorway. He wondered what was going through her mind, if it was as arousing as what was going through his. She closed the door, and he walked to the ladder.

When he entered the kitchen, only Meg sat at the table sipping iced tea with the kitten sleeping in her lap. "Lily and Ned?" he asked.

"They've already eaten. Lily left a note saying she's resting and the sandwiches are in the refrigerator. I don't know what happened to Ned."

"I saw him heading to the side of the house with the pruning shears."

Meg waved to the plate of sandwiches on the table and the bowl of potato salad. "Help yourself."

Unfortunately she was talking about the food.

After washing his hands at the sink, he pulled out the chair across from her. Lifting the glass of iced tea, he drank half of it.

Meg refilled his glass from the pitcher.

The kitten meowed in disapproval as she woke him by changing position.

"What's your friend's name?"

"Leo. I thought he looked like a lion cub when I found him."

"You found him?"

"Out in the bushes one day, scared as could be. He was too little to have gotten here on his own. I think someone dropped him by the road, and he hid in the bushes."

"You care, Meg. Do you know what a valuable quality that is?"

She petted the kitten, soothing and caressing. "Whatever I know, I learned from Aunt Lily and Uncle Ned."

"Maybe. But I think some of it's innate. A magic touch that can't be bought or learned."

Raising her head, she fixed him with a probing stare. "You know what I think?"

He shifted on his chair. "I'm not sure I want to know."

"Well, I'll tell you anyway. You expect yourself to do everything right, best, the perfect way. Don't you think you're expecting too much?"

"I could ask you the same thing."

Scooping up the kitten, she stood and came around to him. "You talk about being realistic. Let's try it." Gently she set Leo in Logan's lap.

"What are you doing?"

She didn't answer.

The kitten padded from Logan's left thigh to his right, looked up and meowed.

"Now what?" Logan growled. "He'd rather be on your lap."

"I'm the interpreter, not you. He's saying he'd like you to pet him."

Logan frowned and lowered his hand to his lap. Leo went to it and rubbed his head against Logan's thumb. When Logan gently rubbed the kitten's cheek, Leo licked his finger.

Logan chuckled. "What do you want? I'm sure Meg feeds you." He tore a tiny piece of cheese from the slice in his sandwich and held it on the pad of his thumb. Leo nibbled it into his mouth, then kept licking Logan's finger. When no more cheese was forthcoming, he rolled his head against Logan's palm.

"What do you feel, Logan?" Meg asked softly.

He felt protective of the small animal. The feeling came from the same source as his protective streak that ran deep for his son. Logan thought back to the night Travis was born. He remembered it as if it were yesterday. He'd offered his son his finger, and Travis had gripped it. The action might have been reflexive, but it had meant everything to Logan. He'd wanted to protect his son with a fierceness that remained through the years. But Travis had run away from him and his caring. It was obvious he'd failed not only as a husband, but as a father, too.

He lifted the kitten from his lap and held it out to Meg. "It doesn't matter."

She took Leo and cuddled him to her breast. "Yes, it does, Logan. You're a caring man."

"You haven't known me very long."

"I know enough."

And he knew if she kept looking at him like that, he'd kiss her again. "Before this conversation gets us both in trouble, I think we'd better eat lunch."

Shaking her head, she returned to her chair. "You and Travis are more alike than you know."

He didn't ask her what she meant, but picked up his sandwich.

Chapter Eight

Not knowing if her idea would cause trouble or make an important point, Meg rang Logan's doorbell late Sunday morning and shifted the wicker basket from her left hand to her right.

When Logan opened the door and saw her standing there, a slow smile spread across his face. "Are you inviting me on a picnic?"

"Not exactly. Can I come in?"

His smile faded, and he motioned her into the living room.

She slipped by him, her elbow brushing his stomach. Although he wore a T-shirt, she could vividly imagine his bare chest, the way his skin had felt under her hands, the texture of his hair. She was afraid too many impressions of Logan were burned into her mind forever. Pages of newspaper strayed across the couch as if Logan had been reading it when she'd rung the bell. The rest of the room was as orderly as she'd seen it before.

Carefully setting the wicker basket down in front of the coffee table, she knelt beside it. "I brought you a present."

"Some of Lily's apple dumplings?"

"Nope. Something a little more fun." She unlatched the basket, and before she could open the lid, Leo's head popped out. He took a look around and meowed.

Meg opened both sides of the basket. "I have a few more things in the car to bring in." Before Logan could recover from his surprise, she escaped out the door.

When she returned, Logan stood, hands on hips, watching the kitten as he meowed and rubbed against his sneaker. Logan's gaze found hers, and his scowl was fierce. "What do you think you're doing?"

"Giving you a gift, including supplies. Where do you want the litter box?" She set it on the floor, removing the sack of litter and the small cans of cat food.

"I don't want it anywhere. I don't want a cat."

"Why not?"

"Because I'm not here most of the time."

Leo clawed up Logan's jeans to his knee. He gently pulled the kitten away from the material and handed him to Meg. "Here. It found a good home with you."

She folded her arms and wouldn't accept the kitten. "He'll find a good life here with you." Ignoring the irritation emanating from Logan, she went to the kitchen. "Is it all right if I find a dish for water? I feed him one-third of a can three times a day." When Logan didn't answer her, she opened a cupboard and found a dish on her own.

He strode into the kitchen after her, the kitten nestled in the crook of his arm. ''What kind of point are you trying to make?''

''No point.''

''You're a lousy liar.''

She snapped the cupboard shut. ''What point do you think I'm trying to make?''

''You think if I'm successful taking care of this cat, I won't feel so frustrated about Travis. The one has nothing to do with the other.''

''Humor me. Try it for a week.''

''I'm not here that much,'' he protested again.

''Cats are independent. They can occupy themselves. Give him some tinfoil balls, tie a string to the chair, he'll be happy. Oh, and don't forget to pet him. Between you and Travis, he'll get plenty of attention.''

''Meg, read my lips. I don't want a cat.''

Meg couldn't suppress her grin as she stood there watching Logan and Leo. Logan's combative stance and tone, as well as his annoyance, directly contradicted the picture of the kitten snuggled against his chest. ''I knew he'd like you.''

Logan swore, lifted Leo and set him on the floor.

Meg filled a saucer with water. ''Should I put his dish by the table?'' She didn't wait for him to answer, but set the saucer on the floor in an out-of-the-way spot by the wall. Leo came over to investigate. When she stood, Logan was right there, the intent to argue with her and win creasing his brow.

He hadn't shaved. Beard stubble darkened his jaw, and she longed to run her fingers along its outline. His hair was rumpled as if he hadn't yet bothered to comb it or else he'd run his fingers through it many times. He looked rakish and altogether too sexy for her to stay in his house alone with him for very long.

"One week, Logan. Let Leo live here for a week before you make a decision."

He clasped her shoulders. "You are one exasperating woman."

Just the weight of his hands on her shoulders excited her, urged her to raise her lips to his for a kiss. But she knew better. Instead, she retorted, "And you are one very stubborn man. You really aren't even supposed to think about giving back a gift."

He slid his hands from her shoulders to her neck and rubbed his thumbs along her jaw. "*You* are a gift."

Her mouth went dry, her heart raced and everything inside her screamed for his kiss and his touch. "Don't be silly."

"What's silly is the two of us arguing about a cat when we could be doing something much more satisfying."

"Logan..."

"Tell me you don't want me to kiss you."

She could hardly catch her breath, but she managed to say, "I can't."

He tilted her chin up and stared deep into her eyes...into her heart. "I'm glad you came into my life. You've brought me light and smiles and passion I forgot I once had."

His low, murmured words aroused her as much as his hand on her face. She swayed toward him and his desire.

Every one of Logan's kisses was different. She never knew what to expect. He didn't home in on her lips, but targeted the soft spot behind her ear. She wrapped her arms around his neck so she wouldn't fall.

She felt him smile against her neck, then he murmured, ''You like that, don't you?''

''Yes.''

He chuckled and kissed her there again. ''I like a woman who knows her mind.'' He stroked down her back, cupped her bottom and brought her tight against him.

Not caring if she was acting wanton, she kissed his jaw and searched for his lips. Logan groaned deep in his throat when she found them. But he wouldn't let her kiss him. He pecked at her nose, softly kissed her cheek, drove her crazy with teasing nips that only made her want to kiss him more. Time stood still as she grabbed at his shoulders, aware of the bunched muscles under her hands, the passion stringing his body tighter and tighter. She could feel that same passion coiling inside her. With each heartbeat, she became more aware of her needs—to be treated, wanted and loved for herself, not for what she did or said or accomplished. Logan's desire for her opened a new world, more adventurous than traveling, more difficult than interpreting. It asked her to give more than her knowledge and talent. It asked her, no—demanded—that she give herself, all she was, maybe all she could be.

When Logan finally set his lips on hers and demanded to taste her, she accepted the demand because she wanted the satisfaction, too. Because when he tasted her, aroused her, consumed her, she could taste, arouse and consume him. Give and take. Equal to equal. Man to woman. Woman to man. She didn't have to worry about being good enough or pleasing him or responding too eagerly because Logan obviously understood her needs and answered them with his.

He slowed the darting of his tongue and hers, prolonging the strokes and prolonging the pleasure. Lost in the rocking of their bodies, the intensity of a kiss that was fast becoming too much to control, Meg heard a noise but didn't let it register. She didn't want anything to interfere; she didn't want...

A louder noise made Logan tear away. He swore under his breath, and Meg didn't understand until she heard someone say, "Not bad, Sheriff MacDonald. Do you give lessons?"

Meg vaguely recognized the voice. With Logan's arm still surrounding her, she opened her eyes. Travis stood in the living room with one of his friends, looking embarrassed and angry at the same time. He gave his friend a push. "Go back to my room. I'll be there in a minute."

Kyle didn't follow directions. "I'd rather stay here and watch."

The muscles in Logan's arm tightened, and so did his jaw. "You know you're not welcome here, Kyle."

"That was before Travis took off. I thought maybe you'd changed your mind."

Travis gave Kyle a "keep quiet" look and challenged his father. "He's my friend. I want him here."

"And I want you to stay out of trouble. If you're with him, you won't."

"I don't pick your friends. You don't get to pick mine."

Neither of the MacDonalds was about to back down. Meg thought about intervening, but before she could, Leo darted into the living room and clawed his way onto the sofa.

Travis looked at the kitten. "What's that?"

Meg smiled and stepped away from Logan's arm. "That's your new housemate. Think you can take good care of him?"

Travis shrugged. "Yeah, I guess so." He turned back to Logan. "Look, Dad. Kyle and I can listen to a new CD here or we can go over to his place. It's your call."

Meg knew Logan hated being backed into a corner.

His voice was rough when he finally said, "All right. You can stay here. But I'm warning you both, stay on the straight and narrow or I'll come down on you so fast your heads will spin."

Kyle saluted Logan with a smile. "Yes, sir."

Travis gave his friend a vigorous shove. "Go. Before you get us both thrown in jail."

Logan watched the boys take off down the hall. "I don't trust Kyle. Not for a minute. I picked him up for shoplifting last year. Before Travis ran off, I caught the two of them drinking."

"Travis must see something he likes in Kyle."

Logan shook his head. "Kyle's dad left when he was ten. His mom's having a hard time making ends meet."

"Maybe Travis senses a loneliness in Kyle that he feels. Losing a parent is tough."

"I never thought of it that way."

Meg crossed to the couch. Now that she and Logan were alone again, she felt awkward about their kiss. "Do you think Kyle will spread around what he saw?"

Logan followed her. "Do you mind if he does?"

She petted Leo, who'd fallen asleep on the couch. "It won't affect me. I don't live here. You do."

"I don't give a damn about what anyone says. Why should I?"

"No, I guess you wouldn't. Things like that enhance a man's reputation."

He took her by the arm. "I don't have a reputation. Not for that. Between grieving, keeping Travis in line and working, I haven't had time for much else."

"There hasn't been anyone since Shelley?"

"No."

"Not even—?"

"Anything casual? I know better. What about you?"

She realized now how insulting the question sounded. Logan wasn't the type of man to take anything casually. "I'm sorry I asked. I..."

His voice was husky when he responded, "You can ask me anything you want. That doesn't mean I'll answer, but you can ask."

The two sides of Logan fascinated her. One side was hard and demanding; the other was compassionate and gentle. She'd guess the one protected the other. "I'd better go."

"So Leo and I can get to know each other better?"

She smiled and walked to the door. "Something like that." Opening the door, she shot over her shoulder, "One more thing, Leo likes to sleep with someone. So you might find him nestled at your feet in the morning."

Behind her, she heard Logan grumble, "That'll be the day." Thinking about being anywhere near Logan's bed tempted her to stay rather than leave. It was

IMPORTANT BEFORE MAILING...

1. Did you play your Zodiac Chart Game and Lucky Star Game? Did you print your name and address on the Game?

2. Did you play the Reach For The Moon Game for free books and a free gift?

PERF OUT AND PLACE HALF OF $50 BILL HERE

Limit one 1st 50 award per household.

Good Luck!

WHAT'S YOUR SIGN?

ZODIAC WHEEL

GEMINI May 21-June 21 · TAURUS Apr. 20-May 20 · ARIES Mar. 21-Apr. 19 · PISCES Feb. 20-Mar. 20 · AQUARIUS Jan. 20-Feb. 18 · CAPRICORN Dec. 22-Jan. 19 · SAGITTARIUS Nov. 22-Dec. 21 · SCORPIO Oct. 24-Nov. 21 · LIBRA Sept. 23-Oct. 23 · VIRGO Aug. 22-Sept. 22 · LEO July 23-Aug. 22 · CANCER June 22-July 22

INSTRUCTIONS:
Locate **your** Zodiac Sign above. Carefully detach and stick it in the space provided on your "ZODIAC CHART GAME" in alignment with your **"1,000,000.00 ALL-CASH WINDFALL!"** Your sign could bring you **your** luckiest numbers ever!

GO FOR AN EXTRA $50 FAST CASH — NOW!

Can you find the other half of this $50 bill? This offer is time sensitive–So be sure to respond <u>NOW</u>–you could be one of 50 drawn who will AUTOMATICALLY receive $50– IN GOOD OLD AMERICAN CASH! To play, detach this half of the $50 bill, moisten it and stick it in the space provided beside the other half. SEE BACK OF BOOK FOR CONTEST DETAILS.

PLAY YOUR ZODIAC SIGN FOR A CHANCE TO WIN $1,000,000.00!

"$1,000,000.00 ALL-CASH WINDFALL!"

WERE YOU BORN TO WIN $1,000,000.00?

SEE INSIDE...

much safer to go back to Aunt Lily's and help her make lunch.

Meg sat on the porch with Lily and Ned on Tuesday evening. When the phone rang, she automatically hopped up, said, "I'll get it" and ran into the house so her aunt and uncle didn't have to jump up.

In the kitchen, she plucked the receiver from its cradle. "Hello."

"I have a bone to pick with you."

Logan's deep voice rolled through her like thunder at midnight. "And what would that be?"

"There's a furry little animal at my house who thinks he owns the place. He claws up the curtains like they're ladders made for him to get to the window."

"You'll have to teach him he can't do that."

"Which method do you propose I try? Lifting him off each time he does it and telling him no, distracting him or yelling? None of them work."

She muffled a giggle.

"I heard that," he scolded.

"You could fill a spray bottle with water and give him a little spritz each time. That should do it."

"You're serious."

"Very serious."

He sighed. "I suppose you also have a remedy for the scratch marks he makes on the furniture when he can't quite get where he wants to go."

"Logan, what are you doing to Leo? He was perfectly behaved when he lived here."

"I'll just bet he was. That's probably why you gave him away."

"Are you questioning my motives?" she teased, thinking he was protesting his dismay just a mite too forcefully.

"No, I'm just questioning what spell you cast over me to get me to agree to keeping him here."

"No spell. Honest."

Logan's voice lowered. "You know you never answered my question."

"Which question?"

"Is there someone special waiting for you in D.C.? Or anywhere else, for that matter?"

"No."

"Why not?"

"Because I tried it once and was very disappointed."

"Tell me."

"Logan..."

"Meg, I want to know. Someone as intelligent and pretty as you could have several special someones."

"He was a journalist. His career was more important than I was."

"According to you or according to him?"

The same anger she'd once felt resurfaced. "I was a convenience, not a partner. If a story broke while we were making love, he had his clothes on faster than he could say goodbye. And when he was out of sight, I was out of his mind. I deserve better."

"Yes, you do." After a long pause, Logan finally said, "I've never been kissed by a woman the way you kiss me. So I can't help but wish you'd be here longer than Thanksgiving."

His words scared her and excited her.

"Meg?" he asked.

"Yes?"

"I'll be over Saturday to finish the roof. Will you be there?"

"Where else would I be?"

"Avoiding me."

Making a decision, she said softly, "I won't avoid you."

"Good. I'll see you then."

When Meg hung up the phone, she smiled. She was looking forward to Saturday.

The following morning, Meg sat in Victoria Lee's office, which resembled professional offices that Meg had seen all over the world with its wood, quality fabrics and computer system. But Victoria Lee *was* her office. Her beautiful, long black hair, her poise, the culture in her voice impressed Meg. So did her forthrightness.

"We always need more help. We have two psychologists on staff who help parents and children in transition. We have two secretaries who set up appointments, take phone calls and try to keep up with the paperwork and copying."

"Does your liaison travel?"

"Now and then. But these days, most of the work is done by phone and fax. It's not a glamorous job. Most of it consists of red tape and bureaucracy. But you would meet with the parents and children, and I can assure you the work is rewarding."

"I imagine it is."

"But you are not ready to commit yourself."

"Miss Lee...."

"'Victoria,' please."

"Victoria, I like the work I do now. At least, I used to."

Victoria's eyes were filled with a wisdom beyond her thirty-some years. "But the experience you went through has given you doubts."

"Not doubts exactly. The point is I'm not going to know how I feel about going back until I'm back. Do you understand?"

She nodded. "Completely. I just don't want you to give me a definite no. I've checked into your background. I know your skills and your reputation. So I wondered if you would consider another option for the time being."

"Such as?"

"As I said, we always need help. How would you feel about putting in some time here, seeing how we work?"

"Could I volunteer?" Time was beginning to lie heavy on Meg's hands. Her energy level was increasing every day, and helping Lily around the house just wasn't enough.

"If you wish, though I'd feel as if we were taking advantage of you."

"No, you wouldn't be. It would give me something worthwhile to do with my time."

Victoria smiled. "That would be fine with me. Why don't you work out a schedule and call me. We'll go from there."

Meg felt good about this meeting, about Victoria Lee's agency, about her decision to help. Working would make her feel useful again.

Meg stood at the bottom of the ladder propped against the garage, a glass of lemonade in hand. Shading her eyes with her hand against the mid afternoon sun, she called up to Logan, "Would you like something cold to drink?"

Logan carefully made his way toward Meg and descended the ladder. His hair had been tossed by the breeze. He wore a shirt today, but he'd unfastened the buttons. The flaps lay on either side of his belt buckle. She couldn't keep her gaze from following the line of dark hair under the snap of his jeans.

"Would you like to touch it?"

His question held a sexy rasp that snapped her eyes to his. She felt the heat crawl into her cheeks and she felt like fanning herself.

"Sorry. I couldn't resist," he said, his smile sly.

He didn't look one bit sorry. "How's Leo?"

Logan tapped her nose. "You're changing the subject."

She tried to keep her expression bland, the idea of touching Logan a passing fancy. "Just checking to see if my little friend has a permanent home."

Logan took the glass of lemonade from her, lifted it to his lips and drank it. The strong muscles of his neck, the stubborn line of his jaw, drew her gaze as easily as the hair on his chest and his flat stomach. When he finished, he handed her the glass. "Your little friend is a pain in the butt. But I'm getting used to him. We have a deal. If he doesn't pounce on the morning paper while I'm trying to read it, I let him lick my cereal bowl."

Meg laughed. "And he understands this deal?"

Logan grinned. "Sure does."

"And where does he sleep?"

"Anywhere he wants. But if you mean at night, I've caught him curled up with Travis."

Meg's smile grew broader.

"Stop looking so smug or I'll have to kiss you, and that's not a good idea here in broad daylight. Considering what happened last time."

"Did Travis say anything?"

"No. But then, he doesn't say much. He goes to school, closets himself in his room in the evenings and stays out till curfew on weekends."

She could see Logan wanted more from his son but didn't know how to go about getting it.

"Speaking of curfews, how would you like to break a few and go dining and dancing with me tonight?" he suggested.

"Tonight?"

"Don't tell me you need more than an afternoon to get ready, because I won't believe it."

"What if I tell you I don't have a thing to wear?"

He arched his brows, and his jaw tensed. "You might as well tell me you'd rather not go."

"Logan, I'm not turning you down. I'm serious."

He stepped closer and pushed her hair behind her ear. "I want to take you dancing and hold you in my arms. For starters."

If she went tonight, she was agreeing to let him into her life. If she went tonight . . . "I could go shopping at Sally's Boutique this afternoon."

"Could?"

The hope in his voice as well as the desire in his eyes encouraged her to make the decision. "I will. What time should I be ready?"

"Seven?"

"Seven's fine. I'll see you then." She turned toward the house.

But Logan's voice stopped her. "Meg, I don't care what you wear."

One look into his eyes told her he'd prefer if she wore nothing at all. She hurried to the house, her cheeks hot, her hands trembling.

Meg had seen lots of men in suits, probably more than she could ever count. But Logan in a suit was a sight to behold. When she opened the door to him, he filled the doorway—broad shoulders in a charcoal jacket, long legs seemingly even longer in the pleated dress slacks. The steel gray shirt underneath looked like silk, and the gray, white and black tie was perfectly knotted. Despite the *GQ* look, he oozed the same sensual masculine appeal as when he wore his uniform or jeans.

Fingering her Aunt Lily's pearls in her ears, she opened the screen door.

Logan stepped inside. His green eyes glinted with golden sparks in the dim foyer light. "You might need a jacket . . . or something."

His gaze lingered on her bare shoulders. The black halter dress that she'd bought at Sally's with its wide cummerbund waist and straight skirt was a basic asset to her wardrobe. She could wear it out to dinner or to an embassy reception. Picking up a black fringed shawl folded over the banister, she asked, "Will this do?"

He took it from her and unfolded it. "Let me help you."

She turned her back to him.

Logan carefully laid it over her shoulders, then bent close to her ear. "I like your hair like this."

His breath at her cheek, his lips so close to her skin, escalated the anticipation inside her to an all-time high. She closed her eyes and tried to calm all the nerves that were rioting out of control.

He fingered a tendril of hair that had escaped the upswept hairdo. "You smell like Lily's rose garden after nightfall."

Before she did something impulsive like turning around and kissing him without caring what he thought about it, she took a deep breath.

He placed a teasing kiss on the nape of her neck and asked, "Are you ready?"

Hoping she wasn't acting like a teenager, knowing she might get hurt, she faced him and said, "I'm ready."

His slow, sexy smile didn't reassure her, but made her heart pound faster.

Logan drove to the Garden, the only choice for dining and dancing in Willow Valley. He had a vision of how he expected this night to end, although he hadn't worked out the practicalities. It was ironic that two adults couldn't find a place to spend time alone, but with Travis at home and Lily and Ned watching over Meg, they might have to rent a hotel room. The problem was he couldn't do that without everyone in Willow Valley gossiping about it.

Lily and Ned's barn was looking better and better.

He pulled into the parking lot of the restaurant and switched off the ignition. Meg's silence indicated her uncertainty about being with him. "Having second thoughts?"

She smiled. "No. Just a bit jittery for our first public appearance. You know people are going to talk."

"About two friends having a quiet dinner together?"

Meg's pretty brows arched.

He took her hand and stroked her knuckles. "I don't care about rumors or what people say."

"I was thinking about Travis and how he might feel."

Logan sighed and stared out the windshield. "Just for tonight, let's not discuss Travis, okay?" He turned and tried to see her expression in the shadows. "Let's just concentrate on us."

Meg reached over and laid her hand on his thigh. The simple overture revved him up until all he thought about was hauling her into his arms and kissing her until she begged him to bury himself in her. But he knew he had to take tonight slowly... if it killed him.

He picked up her hand and brought it to his lips. When he kissed her palm, he felt her tremble. This was going to be one very long, torturous dinner.

Logan learned several things about Meg while they ate. She didn't rush anything—not drinking her wine, not cutting her chicken *cordon bleu,* not chewing and savoring each bite. She was a careful person, but she knew how to enjoy herself, she knew how to relax, she knew how to drive him crazy from wanting her by simply being herself.

The table's breadth separated them, and he hated the distance. Yet the brush of his knee against hers, the answering expectation in her eyes, aroused him as completely as holding her in his arms.

They didn't talk much. They gazed into each other's eyes a lot. Every once in a while, she gave him a shy smile, and he stroked her hand. This kind of foreplay was new to him and erotic as hell.

The four-piece orchestra began playing as they sipped coffee. Finally Logan couldn't stand sitting across from Meg when he wanted to feel her pressed against him. He pushed back his chair, stood and held out his hand to her. "C'mon. Let's dance."

She placed her hand in his with a smile that could make a stormy sky turn blue. Logan protectively curved his arm around her and led her to the dance floor.

Taking Meg in his arms seemed as natural as breathing. At first he left a few inches between them. Her brown eyes locked to his were enough. But slowly, with each heartbeat, he drew her closer...too close to dance, almost too close to breathe.

Her hand slipped out of his, and she linked her arms around his neck. He caressed her bare back, feeling the tremors course through her. Smiling, he rested his jaw against her temple, savoring the response of a beautiful woman in his arms.

After Travis was born, sex had been a duty to Shelley, a duty she'd used for her own benefit. She'd used her pregnancy and their hasty marriage as grounds to keep her distance. And he'd been a fool to believe commitment could stand in for feelings that had never matured or deepened. As always, Logan tried to push the guilt away and didn't succeed.

Meg released a soft sigh, and her breasts pushed against his chest. The lightning-quick response of his body had to be obvious. But she didn't pull away.

He brought his hand to the back of her neck and rubbed in a small circle. Lifting her chin, she waited.

Bending his head, he kissed her. The music wound about them, her perfume intoxicated him and her taste aroused him. They were the only two people in the world, and all he could think about—

Beep, beep...beep, beep.

Beep, beep...beep, beep.

Meg pulled back.

Logan swore. "I told Cal not to page me unless he had an emergency. I have to call."

He escorted Meg to their table, then went to the phone at the reception desk. "Cal? This had better be good. What's going on?"

"Someone broke into the high school. You'd better get over here."

Logan looked over at the table where Meg sat. So much for the night he'd planned. Damn. He had to shut down his libido and wake up his sixth sense instead of his baser ones. "I'll be there in fifteen minutes. Don't touch anything."

"I know better than that."

"Sorry, Cal. I'll get there as soon as I can."

"You droppin' Meg Dawson off first?"

Logan sighed. He wasn't going to even ask how his deputy knew. There were few secrets in Willow Valley. "Yes, I am."

He hung up and crossed to Meg. Usually he liked his work. Usually, he didn't hesitate to go when duty called. But tonight *duty* was a four-letter word he'd rather wipe from his vocabulary.

Chapter Nine

An hour later, Logan stood in the principal's office, waiting for Michael Holden to answer his question.

Michael ran his hand through his brown hair. "The change is gone from the cafeteria office. Fifty dollars. The individual classrooms don't seem to have anything missing. Do you want me to call the teachers tomorrow and have them come in and check?"

Logan surveyed Michael's office for the tenth time, interested in anything that might look suspicious or out of place. "That would probably be a good idea. What about in here?"

"I keep it locked—too much confidential information."

Logan peered into the full waste can. "When does the janitor clean?"

"Early Monday morning while I'm in the building."

Logan respected the way Michael ran the school. "But he cleans the rest of the school on Saturday?"

"That's right."

Logan rubbed his chin. "From what I can tell, I think the thief snuck in this afternoon while the janitor was cleaning. Mrs. Konnecut saw someone leaving by the west door, and that's why she called us."

"Did she recognize who it was?"

"No. And she keeps track of everything and everyone she can. But her sight is failing. Cal's at her place now. I'm going to stop there to question her, too, and to see if I can pick up any more details. Do you have any ideas who broke in?"

"Not offhand. But I'll circulate Monday and have the teachers keep their ears open. If someone did it for a prank or a dare, he'll brag."

"No one tampered with your office door."

"And that means...?" Michael asked.

"I think it means the thief thought your office would be too much trouble. He wanted easy pickings and he probably knew where to get them."

Logan walked out into the main office area and narrowed his eyes, staring at the computer on the secretary's desk, the long counter where students stood to wait for information or directions. He'd gone over everything at least ten times.

Michael followed, going behind the counter and looking over the area again.

"I'll come in tomorrow and talk to your teachers. There's nothing more we can do here now," Logan decided.

Michael crossed to the door and switched off the light, then walked with Logan down the hall. "The school is updated but old. I've debated about getting an estimate on a security system, but it's never been necessary. But after this break-in, I'm sure someone will bring it before the board.''

"I hate to see Willow Valley change, but we're getting bigger. Now some people do lock their doors. It's reality.'' Logan checked his watch. Eleven o'clock. Even if he didn't have to interview Mrs. Konnecut, it was too late to pick up the evening where he and Meg had left off.

Michael locked the front door of the school. "Cal said you and Meg Dawson were having dinner when he paged you.''

Logan swore. "I might as well have taken out an ad. I'd like to know where Cal found out in the first place.''

Michael grinned. "It seems a friend of his wife talked to Meg when she was buying a dress for the occasion.''

Logan shook his head.

"So you and Meg are going out now?'' Michael asked, his interest obviously more than casual.

"That's my intention,'' Logan responded, jealousy pricking at him. He had no doubt if he was out of the picture, Holden would make a move of his own.

Michael shrugged. "Just checking. She's an intriguing woman.''

"That she is.'' Logan wasn't about to discuss anything about himself and Meg.

The two men descended the steps and went to their cars. Logan called to Michael, "After I stop at Mrs. Konnecut's, I'm going to the office to file a report. If you think of anything else you think I need to know, I'll be there.''

Michael opened his car door. "Good luck.''

"With Mrs. Konnecut?"

"With Mrs. Konnecut and with Meg."

Logan didn't quite know what to say to that, so he got into his car. He couldn't ever remember a rival wishing him good luck. Either Michael Holden was a genuinely nice guy or a man to watch. Logan decided he'd better watch.

Only a few minutes of daylight remained when Meg saw Logan's car coming down the lane. He'd dropped her off last night with a quick but thoroughly devastating goodbye kiss that she'd felt long after he'd gone. The evening had been exciting and perfect up until the moment when Logan's pager had beeped. She could read his disappointment as they'd hastily ended their date as much as she could feel her own.

Yet maybe Providence had intervened. Maybe she wasn't supposed to get involved with Logan any more than she already was.

"Looks like you've got company," Ned remarked with a sly wink as he hung a lawn chair on a hook in the garage. When he'd told her he wanted to clean out and straighten up, she'd offered to help to keep herself busy. Her uncle added, "We can finish this tomorrow."

"Maybe Logan's here to visit you and Lily."

Her uncle chucked her under the chin. "You're a lot younger and prettier than we are. I don't think there's any doubt as to who he's here to see. But Lily and I will be inside if you two younger folks need the wisdom of a few years." Ned waved to Logan as he walked toward the back door.

Meg rounded her uncle's car and met Logan at the path to the house.

She smiled.

He smiled.

Then he pulled her into his arms for a hug. "Do you know how difficult it was to leave you last night?"

"I can guess."

He rubbed his chin against the top of her head. "I was tied up all day today at the school."

Leaning back in his arms, she asked, "Did you find out anything more?"

"Not much. Nothing else was missing. Mrs. Konnecut thinks she saw a blond teenager in jeans, but she admits her cataracts make her unsure."

"You don't have much to go on."

"No, but Michael thinks scuttlebutt will produce information."

"The kids respect him. If anyone knows anything, they might tell him outright."

Logan shook his head. "They won't snitch on each other. Not at that age. It's their code of honor."

Silence fell between them. Logan's gaze left hers, drifted over her nose, settled on her lips. "What do you think of Michael Holden?"

It was the last question she expected. With a shrug, she said, "Michael is—"

"Meg! Logan! Come here quick. Something's wrong with Lily," Ned yelled from the porch, waving his arms.

Meg and Logan both took off at a run. Logan got to Lily first. The older woman was sitting on the sofa, as pale as the white doily on the coffee table. Perspiration stood on her forehead, and she clutched her chest.

Logan helped Lily stretch out on the sofa. Pulling the afghan from the back, he covered her with it. Then he said to Meg, "Open her collar. I'm going to make sure the rescue squad is at home base. If not, I'll take her to the hospital myself."

Ned stood by, helpless, his face stricken, as Logan made the call. Afterward he slammed down the phone and crouched down beside Meg's aunt. "Hold on, Lily. They'll be here in about four minutes."

It was the longest four minutes of Meg's life. She and Logan encouraged Lily, making her as comfortable as possible as Ned held her hand. Logan went outside when he heard the siren. In a matter of minutes, paramedics transported Lily to the rescue van. Logan drove Ned and Meg to the hospital in Lynchburg.

After what seemed like an eternity in the waiting area of the emergency room, Ned dropped his head into his hands. "Meg, what am I going to do if something happens to her? She's my life!"

Meg laid a comforting hand on her uncle's shoulder although her fears mirrored his. She couldn't imagine life without her aunt. "She's a fighter. You know that. Heart attacks don't have to be fatal. There's so much medicine can do now."

Logan had been calm and collected since Ned had called to him. He stoically sat next to Meg, waiting with them. Abruptly he stood. "I'll see what I can find out. Flashing a badge might help." He strode off before Meg could thank him.

When he returned, he said, "They've taken her up to the coronary-care unit. Doc Jacobs is already up there."

Meg felt tears prick her eyes. "Did you call him?"

"From my car after the paramedics arrived. I thought a friendly face might help."

Trying to blink the tears away, Meg said, "Thank you."

Logan curved his arm around her shoulders. "Let's go upstairs."

A nurse motioned Ned and Meg to a small private waiting area. Doc Jacobs stood by the sofa.

Logan said, "I'll wait outside."

Meg took his hand. "I'd like you to stay, but it's up to you."

He rubbed his thumb across the top of her knuckles. "Whatever you want."

Doc Jacobs cleared his throat. "I spoke to the cardiologist. He was called back to the emergency room. He'll be glad to talk to you later if you'd like." The doctor gestured to the sofa. "Why don't we sit?"

Ned sat but said, "Just tell us, Doc."

Logan guided Meg to the cushion beside her uncle.

"Lily did have a heart attack, but we believe the damage is minimal. We are, of course, going to watch her very closely, especially the next twenty-four hours. She is stabilized for now, and I'm hoping that status won't change. But the human body is unpredictable. The cardiologist wants to wait until tomorrow before he makes a decision about further tests."

"Will she have to have a heart bypass? You've got to do everything you can...."

Compassion glowed in Doc's eyes. "We *are* doing everything possible. And we're taking good care of her. You can go in to see her, but only for fifteen minutes. I'll be able to answer your questions better tomorrow, and so will the cardiologist. I want you to stay calm so Lily stays calm. Understand?"

Both Ned and Meg nodded.

"All right. Then let's go tell her to rest so she doesn't think she's the one who has to take care of everyone else."

Meg and Ned followed Doc to the cubicle where her aunt lay. After kissing Lily, holding her hand for a few minutes and murmuring hopeful thoughts, Meg said to her uncle, "I'll let you spend the rest of the time alone with her."

Meg stepped outside the cubicle and immediately started shivering. Winding her arms around herself, she put one foot in front of the other and walked toward the waiting area. She stopped inside the door and leaned against the wall.

Logan stood at the window, looking out but not seeing. He recognized the tightness in his gut as the worry that had haunted him all the days he hadn't known Travis's whereabouts. Lily and Ned were as integral to Willow Valley as the World War II monument in the park, as Gibson's Grocery, as the willow trees that had given the town its name. Logan knew nothing in life was permanent. His years as a cop in Philadelphia, Shelley's pregnancy and death, Travis running away, had proved to him again and again that life could turn on a dime.

But somehow the stability of his life in Willow Valley was connected to the people who lived there. And to think of Willow Valley without Lily...

He heard footsteps and turned in time to see Meg sag against the wall. Without a moment's hesitation, he hurried to her and enfolded her in his arms. "Has something happened?"

She shook her head against his shoulders. Her breathing was uneven, and he knew shock had set in.

Stroking her hair, he said, "Let it out, Meg. It's okay. Just let it out."

When sobs shook her, he held her tight.

He couldn't tell her everything would be better in the morning, because he didn't know if it would. So he offered her his physical strength, a shelter for the moment, and hoped that was enough.

Finally, she raised her gaze to his. "I'm sorry."

"There's nothing to apologize for."

"But I have to be strong for them. I can't—"

"You *are* strong. You've had a shock and you're afraid of losing someone important to you." He wiped the tears from her cheek and tugged her toward the sofa. Keeping his arm around her shoulders, he sat with her and waited, never before feeling so protective about a woman.

By the time Ned returned, Meg had composed herself. The straightening of her spine, the squaring of her shoulders, signaled her dependence on Logan for support was about to end.

When Ned came in, she immediately went to him and hugged him. "She's going to be all right. She has to."

He nodded and swiped at the moisture in his eyes. "I'm staying here tonight. Why don't you let Logan take you home?"

"No, I'm staying here with you."

Logan took a deep breath, knowing he was about to fight an uphill battle. "Now, wait a minute. Both of you. How are you going to take care of Lily if you get run-down?"

"Logan, we don't want to be a half hour away," Meg explained.

He offered a solution. "There's a motel—"

"I'm staying right here," Ned said stubbornly.

"And I'm staying with him," his niece agreed.

"You two are a pair."

Ned put his arm around Meg's shoulders. "Family has to stick together."

Logan shook his head. "All right. But at least let me get you some pillows and blankets."

Meg smiled weakly and took Logan's hand. "Those we'll accept."

Logan looked at Ned's arm around Meg, her hand entwined with his, and he felt Lily's presence though physically she lay in another room. He experienced a connection with all of them, a connection he'd really never felt before. Suddenly he had the urge to include Travis in the circle. But he didn't know how.

The sun hadn't yet broken the horizon when Logan took the elevator to the coronary-care unit the following morning. When he entered the waiting room, he found Ned stretched out on the long sofa and Meg curled up on the shorter one. She lay with her hands tucked under her cheek, her elbows close to her body as if she were cold.

Logan set the carrier of coffee, juice and food he'd bought on the low table littered with magazines. Then he pulled Meg's blanket up to her chin, annoyed with himself for thinking about touching her creamy skin and kissing her pink lips when she obviously needed attention of another kind. This was not the time to think about steamy nights, long, wet kisses and satisfaction of his physical needs. Except he couldn't help imagining it and longing for it.

When he smoothed the blanket under her chin, her eyes opened. She propped up on an elbow, trying to orient herself.

Logan crouched down beside her. "Hi, there. Did you get much sleep?"

She smiled. "I'm used to sleeping in strange places. Though usually they're hotel rooms."

He couldn't resist leaning forward and sealing his lips to hers. He meant it as a light, caring gesture, but it took on a life of its own.

Kissing Meg took him on an adventure of self-discovery. He never knew he could need so much, or expect so much, or want something so elusive that the sensation almost terrified him. Even here, kissing her on a waiting-room couch, time stopped, the universe spun and dawn broke through the black night. She'd brought light into his life . . . and forgotten passion.

After breaking away, he tenderly caressed her cheek.

She ran a hand through her hair and sat up. "I'm glad Uncle Ned finally fell asleep. The doctor let him sit with Aunt Lily through some of last night. Those two can't bear to be separated from each other."

"I checked at the desk. Your aunt is sleeping comfortably." He lifted the box from the coffee table. "So how about a little nourishment?"

She wrinkled her nose as if eating was an abhorrent thought.

"Come on. I have a few fast-food breakfast sandwiches and doughnuts."

She looked at the waxy bag with a little more interest.

"Chocolate honey glazed?"

Logan laughed. "Ah-hah. I've discovered the woman's weakness."

"Addiction. I rarely turn down chocolate."

He opened the bag and lifted out the chocolate doughnut and handed it to her. "I'll remember that."

Meg couldn't remember a man ever bringing her breakfast. Logan was dressed in his uniform, his dark brown shirt and tan slacks looking crisp and pressed. "Thank you."

"For stopping for coffee?"

"No. For being here. Last night. This morning. I don't know what's going to happen but..." Her voice caught.

"Hopefully your aunt is going to recover, and life will go on. Will this change your plans for returning to D.C.?"

"I don't know. I'll have to wait and see."

Logan's jaw tightened. He picked up one of the coffees, flipped off the lid and took a few sips. Then he capped it again. "I have to get going. I told Michael I'd drop by the school. My presence might shake up whoever stole the money. I don't want anything worse to happen."

"Worse?"

"If this was a prank, that's one thing. But if someone *needs* money, the crime could escalate. I don't want that to happen. So I'll probably be giving a few lectures on solving problems by looking at all the options rather than taking the easiest one."

"Have you talked to Travis about what happened?"

"He was too occupied with a new CD and headphones."

"Does he know you're going into school today?"

"No. And he's not going to like it, but he'll have to live with it. Call me if there's any news about Lily. They can page me."

Logan seemed to have distanced himself. Because of talk of her leaving? Yet he knew she couldn't stay. She was already making lists, preparing herself to get back into circulation. The reception for the Native American Museum Fund in three weeks would be the perfect opportunity. "The cardiologist said he'd be here around eight. We should know more then. I'll call you."

Logan studied her for a few moments, and she felt self-conscious. What was he thinking? What was he feeling? More than desire?

He nodded to the doughnut. "Don't forget to eat."

"I won't."

He left then, and she felt . . . alone.

The late-morning sun shone on Meg and Lily as they sat on the front porch two weeks later. Meg examined her aunt's face, looking for telltale signs of fatigue or overexertion.

"Uncle Ned will be out here in five minutes to check if you're getting chilled. Are you sure you don't want a sweater?"

Lily frowned. "I love that man dearly, but he's driving me crazy."

Meg chuckled. "You gave us quite a scare."

"I know, but I'm very fortunate. If I take the heart attack as a wake-up call, I can be healthier than before."

The cardiologist had kept Lily in the hospital for a week. At the end of that time, he'd ordered a stress test. The results were encouraging. He'd also ordered a nutritionist to counsel Lily and a cardiac-rehab specialist to explain the types of exercise that would benefit her the most. But life-style changes never came easily.

"Uncle Ned seems to like the new diet."

"Don't you try to pull the wool over my eyes, young lady. He might not mind eating turkey instead of roast beef, but he misses his sweets. I know he snuck off to the bakery yesterday."

"And how do you know that?" Her aunt was right, but Meg felt a certain loyalty toward protecting them both.

"Because when he came home, he had powdered sugar on his shirt!"

Meg laughed. "Uncle Ned should know after all these years he can't hide anything from you."

"What he should know is that he shouldn't try." Her aunt pointed to the lane. "Look who's coming."

Meg didn't have to look. She knew the sound of the sedan's tires on the gravel. The truth was she was perturbed with Logan yet had no right to be. She'd called him from the hospital the day after Lily had been admitted to tell him her aunt's condition. He'd called and spoken to Ned twice since then, not asking for Meg. Meg had decided she wasn't about to call him.

Logan mounted the porch stairs, a bouquet of flowers in his arms. After presenting them to Lily, he sat on the top porch step. "How are you feeling?"

"Fine. But nobody will believe me," she grumbled as she smelled the flowers.

Logan grinned. "You have lots of people who care about you. Let them pamper you a little."

"They're pampering me until I'm suffocating." She pointed to her niece. "This one, for instance, thinks she has to cook and clean and do all the laundry. I'm going to have to get a note from my doctor so she'll let me load the washing machine! She even postponed volunteering at the adoption agency. I told her she's going tomorrow morning if I have to push her out."

Meg shook her finger at her aunt. "Your doctor said no heavy lifting. You're to walk and build up your strength. After your next checkup, we'll talk about the laundry. And we'll talk about tomorrow when tomorrow comes."

Lily looked toward heaven. "She's worse than a drill sergeant." Suddenly a twinkle sparkled in her eyes. "I have a great idea, Logan. Why don't you take her on a picnic? She could use a break."

"I don't need a break," Meg murmured, embarrassed her aunt was backing Logan into a corner.

"See? She's prickly. Meg never gets prickly. So she definitely needs a break," Lily assured Logan with a smile.

Logan's gaze fell on Meg. "Would you like to go on a picnic?"

"I wouldn't want to force you into anything." The comment just sort of popped out.

Logan's brows arched. "No one forces me into anything. If you can find a blanket, we can stop at Gibson's and get what we need. I know the perfect spot."

Logan did know the perfect spot. Laurel grew along the bank of the stream. Willows swayed low, their branches whispering with the breeze. He often drove the few miles out of town and sat on the bank of this stream. He'd thought about seeing Meg again constantly for the past two weeks. But he knew she was distracted at first with worry about Lily and then with her aunt's care.

Logan studied Meg as she pushed her purse to the corner of the blanket. It fell over, and the clasp popped open. Ignoring it, she reached into the deli bag and took out the sandwiches. They'd only talked about what they should buy for lunch. He could sense Meg holding back, and he wanted to get to the bottom of it.

"You've been very quiet."

She raised her gaze to his. "I wasn't sure if you came to visit Lily or me."

He tried to suppress a smile. "Both won't do?"

Avoiding his gaze, she set a turkey sandwich before him. "I haven't seen you for two weeks."

"You were busy. I didn't want to interfere."

"Just say it, Logan. You changed your mind. You lost interest...whatever happens to men when they don't call back."

He clasped her wrist. "Don't lump me with everyone else."

Her gaze locked to his. "Why not if you act the same way?"

"Act the same way? The last date we had, I couldn't keep my hands off you. Why would I lose interest?"

She pulled her hand out of his grasp. "Maybe you finally realized I'm going to leave and someone else could meet your needs better."

The passion inside him for Meg Dawson burst the restraints he'd carefully kept in check. He rose to his knees and cradled her head in his hands. "I want you. No one else. I haven't lost interest. But every time I hear your voice, see you, touch you, I want more. And you didn't have time for more with Lily on your mind.''

He still saw the doubts, the sense of abandonment she carried with her from her childhood. And there was only one way he knew to make that go away.

Pulling her up to him, he sought Meg's lips, and he didn't hold back. With her gasp of surprise, he plunged his tongue into her mouth, intending to erase each of her doubts and assure her he wanted her more than he'd ever wanted anyone.

Chapter Ten

Logan's mouth was possessive and hard on Meg's. He turned his head and, with an urgent thrust, pushed his tongue into her mouth again. The dark sweetness of her increased his need, and the desire to show her that his interest had reached new heights, rather than diminished, was foremost in his mind. He searched and stroked and possessed until her arms wound about his neck, and he was sure she understood that he wanted her in the primal way a man wants a woman.

Suddenly she returned his desire. She took it, made it her own and gave it back to him with flames that licked at his body, intent on consuming him. He groaned, his arousal straining for freedom, his body dying for her touch. But the kiss was too intense to break, the pleasure too great to cut off. He wanted it to go on forever. Yet he knew he couldn't last. He was too close to the edge now.

He breathed in the scent of roses and Meg. Searching her mouth for every bit of sweetness, he ran his hands over her shoulders, down her arms. His senses reeled.

As his fingers danced over her skin, she became more daring. Her tongue dashed to the corner of his lips. When he tried to capture her, she evaded him, kissing his bottom lip, then the upper, then meeting him again lips to lips and tongue to tongue while her fingers dug into his hair.

Logan wrapped his arms around her and stroked her back. He felt the heat under the cotton blouse, and he wanted it at his fingers. He pulled her blouse from her skirt and unhooked her bra. The buttons evaded his trembling fingers as he tried to unfasten them, all the while kissing her harder, trying to assuage some of the need.

The last button tore, but it didn't matter because finally he filled his hands with the softness of her breasts. The sounds she made encouraged him. As he rubbed over her breasts with his thumbs, she bit his lip, and the intensity of their passion was almost a physical blow.

He broke away and, when she cried out in protest, he bent his head to her breast and swirled his tongue around her nipple. She grabbed at his shoulders, and her fingernails dug through his shirt. When he took her nipple between his lips, nipping and nibbling and licking, finally suckling in a mating rhythm that was driving them both insane, she clawed at his shirt, dragging it up his back. Finally her fingers touched his skin, and he shuddered.

Pulling back, he separated from her for only a moment and tugged his shirt over his head. Then he kissed her again, taking her down on the blanket. Her gaze met his, and there was no turning back.

He couldn't get enough of her satin skin, golden in the reflection of the sun's rays. Looking and tasting, he devoured her and coaxed broken moans from her that drove him on. Her breasts swelled under their dusky rose peaks. He bit gently, and she grew more restless, reaching for him, murmuring his name. He felt powerful . . . invincible . . . and whole.

Meg's hands felt like soft, branding instruments of sweet torture as she caressed his chest. When her thumb slid over his nipple, he sucked in a breath and wondered how much more he could take. Her hands danced over his shoulders, his chest, his stomach, in restless abandon. Beads of sweat broke out on his forehead, and his breathing became ragged.

Cupping Meg's head, Logan kissed her with the desperate need building inside him. He searched for the hem of her skirt and brushed it up her thigh. She was silk and heat, and he was dying to plunge himself inside her. But she had to be ready. He had to make her ready.

He nibbled down her neck and stroked her inner thigh. She was so hot there . . . so soft. She undulated toward him, and he explored higher until he met a silky barrier. When he played his fingers over it, she cried out. He dragged in a breath, trying to rein in his body's need. Wherever they were going to go, he had to take her with him. He had to.

Meg couldn't seem to breathe in enough air to help her think coherently. Logan's kiss had started a spiral of desire and need and longing that was taking her somewhere she'd never been. His need was hers; hers was his. There was an intangible connection between them, deeper than the passion lacing their kisses and touches.

Logan's tongue on her nipple brought tears to her eyes. The sensation was so beautifully erotic. His taste and texture and scent were everywhere, surrounding her, making her long for more. But any more would almost be too much, wouldn't it? How much pleasure could she absorb without losing herself in him?

When he cradled her head, and the passion seared the depths of her soul, all she wanted was more of him in her arms. She wanted to feel his body against hers, his skin against hers. He glided his hand up her thigh, and she realized skin against skin would never be enough. She wanted him inside her, touching her core, reaching a place that was isolated... alone...waiting.

When he found the juncture of her thighs, she wanted to touch him as intimately as he was touching her. She reached for his belt buckle. Logan helped her, stripping off his jeans and briefs, coming back to her with a kiss that made her forget they'd been separated even for a moment. As he stretched out on top of her, his hips met hers. She could feel his arousal through her skirt, through her panties, and she wanted no barriers between them.

Arching up to meet him, she could feel more, but not enough. Apparently Logan understood the message. Leaning to the side, he swept up her skirt. But he didn't hurry to undress her. He simply laid his hand over her panties, arousing her until the core of her throbbed.

"Logan!"

"What, sweetheart?" His voice was raspy and deep.

"It's not enough. It's..."

In a deft motion, his long fingers and large hand ridded her of her undergarment. "It's not enough for me, either."

While he kissed her, he caressed her thigh, inching higher and higher. She couldn't stand the anticipation, the waiting, the suspense. She wanted to cry out in frustration. Her body screamed, *More, more, more.* And then his fingers parted her and she felt as if she'd explode. He knew how to touch...and where to touch. She melted around him and kissed him as he took her deeper and deeper into passion and taught her the recklessness of desire.

She clutched at his shoulders, feeling the same glistening slickness on his skin that she felt on hers. The warmth of the sun penetrated the canopy of leaves above them, but she knew that her heat and Logan's came from the two of them together, a ball of fire that ignited inside them when they were together—inside of them, not outside. Her fire and his fire were coalescing into one. When they joined, she was afraid she wouldn't care if she ever burned alone again. There was something magical about their desires uniting, becoming more powerful, fed by each other, so much more together than separate.

The hungry yearning of her body centered in her womb, under Logan's deft fingers. When he found the silky nub, hidden, waiting for him, his touch was so sensually slow and erotic, she cried, "I want you, Logan."

He took her at her word, meeting her hips with his, joining his lips to hers, resting at the entrance where her need for him was greatest. She felt the tip of him, the scalding heat of tangible passion, and knew he was waiting for her consent.

Nothing in this world could stop the fire between them now. Nothing in this world could prevent Meg from giving her heart with her body. Nothing could keep her from raising her hips and inviting Logan to possess her.

And possess her he did. He took her hands and held them above her head. Intertwining his fingers with hers, he murmured, "Raise your knees."

The huskiness in his voice, the green depths of emotion in his eyes, the trembling of their hands that was neither his nor hers but theirs, urged her to do as he demanded.

When she did, he thrust into her with all the power of his need.

"Logan!" The sensation was sublime. She could feel his heat, his heartbeat, his pulsating desire. He withdrew and she protested.

He caught her protest and her breath with a scalding kiss as he thrust into her again.

Quickly she closed her knees and gripped his hips, taking him deeper, prolonging the pleasure. He tore away. "Meg, I can't hold on when you do that. Let me..."

"Don't hold on." She contracted around him, and he groaned. With another powerful thrust, he stoked the fire. Each time he drove into her, she rose to meet him until they moved as one, burning into each other.

The fire became liquid, flashing over her in waves, melding them together. Each wave became more intense than the one before. She couldn't think in words, only in feelings and senses. Logan's taste was on her lips, his scent mingled with hers, surrounding them, his hands closed and opened with hers in cadence with his thrusts. The fire danced in front of her eyes, first red, then orange, then silver white—white heat that licked and swelled and finally burst into an explosion that rocked the universe. She couldn't breathe as the orgasm shook her, subsiding, swelling, subsiding, swelling until the prolonged tremors became Logan's, as well as hers. The ecstasy seemed to last forever.

Finally she needed air, and she drew in a deep breath. Logan's body was still on top of her.

He lifted himself on his forearms. "Are you okay?"

Gazing into his eyes, realizing what had happened, her mind racing ahead, asking *what happens next?* she answered, "I'm not sure."

"I hope you don't have regrets."

How could she regret something so wonderful? Yet...

He frowned and separated from her. "I only have one regret."

"What?"

"Are you on the pill?"

Her eyes widened, and the full impact of his question hit her. "No."

He laid on his back beside her and stared up at the leaves blocking the blue sky. "I wouldn't want either of us to be trapped into something we don't want."

Would she feel trapped? Obviously Logan would. Because of a pregnancy, he'd been trapped in an unhappy marriage. "We should have known better."

"*I* should have known better." He rolled toward her, studied her face and pushed her damp hair from her brow. "But when I'm with you, I feel like a teenager again. Apparently with about just as much sense."

"You don't sound happy about it."

"Are you? Do you burn every time we get within a foot of each other? Does the sound of my voice turn you on? Does an inadvertent touch make you need?"

She heard his frustration, but she heard vulnerability, too. "Logan, yes. I wanted you as much as you wanted me. How could you doubt that after the way I . . . ?"

"Some women can pretend real well."

"Logan!"

"It's true. Shelley—" He stopped.

"Tell me," she requested softly.

He stared up at the leaves above them. Finally he said, "After Shelley became pregnant, she was less than enthusiastic about sex. I thought we just needed time. But after Travis was born, she didn't want any more children. It was always a point of contention between us and colored whatever happened in the bedroom. When we made the decision to move to Willow Valley, I asked her if we couldn't start over, consider having another child. She agreed. After we moved, I thought our marriage was better. She seemed to enjoy sex again. Then I found out it was an act to cover up for her guilt."

Meg moved her leg closer to Logan's. Her arm brushed his. She wanted the physical contact to let him know he could tell her whatever he was thinking and feeling.

"One evening I saw something sticking out of her dresser drawer. I opened the drawer to stuff it back in, and I felt a package at the edge, the reason it wouldn't close. It was a packet of birth-control pills with some missing."

Turning on her side, Meg watched Logan's chest rise and fall and wondered if he'd ever told anyone about any of this or if he'd kept it inside all these years.

"I confronted her with them. We started shouting. Saying things we shouldn't have. I don't even remember them now. But I do remember her telling me she never should have married me—not for a baby's sake. She said I'd ruined her life. Then she ran out, and an hour later I got the call. She was speeding, lost control and ran the car into a telephone pole. She was killed on impact."

Logan's expression manifested anguish, as if it had just happened, as if he blamed himself. Instinctively Meg reached for him and held him tight.

His body was rigid, as if he couldn't accept her comfort. After a few minutes, he kissed her. The sparks burst into flame again, but this time he pulled away. "We'd better not tempt fate twice," he said in a husky murmur. "Let's have lunch."

Meg felt awkward dressing, putting her clothes in order. But as Logan zipped his jeans, he smiled at her. Not sure what he was thinking or feeling, she proceeded cautiously. "Remember I told you I have to go to D.C. for a fund-raiser?"

Logan nodded.

Noticing the top button of her blouse was torn off, she decided not to worry about it. A little cleavage at this point didn't much matter. "It's next weekend. Saturday night. I wondered if you'd like to go along with me as my escort."

"Black-tie?" He buckled his belt.

She couldn't seem to move her gaze from his hands, the fly of his jeans. Her body was still tingling, and the thought of being with him again . . .

"Meg?" The sexy, knowing smile on his face made her blush.

"Uh, yes. It is. We could stay at my apartment."

His smile turned into a full-fledged grin. "I'll have to make sure Travis has somewhere to stay. But he has friends besides Kyle. It shouldn't be a problem. When do you want to leave?"

"Saturday morning around eight?"

"Sounds good." He sat down beside her. "But what sounds even better is a night at your apartment."

"Logan, I don't know where we're headed...."

He caressed her cheek. "I don't, either. But until we get there, let's just enjoy ourselves. Okay?"

She nodded.

Meg couldn't remember when she'd enjoyed an impromptu picnic more. Of course, she'd never been on a picnic quite like this one. She still couldn't believe... She sneaked a surreptitious glance at Logan—at least, she thought it was surreptitious—as he took a bite from an apple. His jaw was so strong and well chiseled. His cheekbones were high. The long lines beside his mouth deepened when he smiled. And his mouth...

He caught her looking, and the green of his eyes deepened. Leaning toward her, he offered her a bite of apple. "It's juicy," he said with a wink.

She'd never thought of Logan as a ladies' man, but she realized he could be devastatingly charming without half an effort. She took a bite and the juice ran down her chin. When she reached for a napkin, Logan took it from her.

"Let me."

Bending to her, he licked the apple juice from her chin. He didn't stop there, but settled his lips on hers.

When he ended the kiss, she wished the picnic would never end.

He smiled. "Would you like the apple? I have another one."

Maybe if she crunched on the fruit, she'd forget about what else they could be doing. She took it from him.

He reached to the corner of the blanket for the grocery bag. Her purse lay open with the contents spilled out. First he picked up the lipstick and tossed it inside. Then he gathered the pen and small notepad. When he glanced at it, he frowned. "What's this?"

She could protest he had no authority to poke into her things, but there was no point to that. "It's a list. I make them all the time. They help me stay organized."

"This one looks important. Names. Numbers. All D.C. area code."

"People I'm going to call next weekend."

"Friends?"

She took the notepad from him and pushed it into her purse. "No, my contacts and colleagues who should know when I'm returning."

"You've made a decision?" There was a strain in his voice.

"I want to make sure Aunt Lily's okay. So I'm going to tell them I'll return January 1."

"You sound sure."

"I am sure."

He lifted her chin. "And what about what happened today? How does that figure in?"

She searched his eyes and her heart. "I don't know."

"Do you think it was a mistake?"

He was forcing her to look at them and make some kind of decision. She had to admit, "Maybe it was. Our roads are different, Logan. I have to go back to my work. You know that."

Dropping his hand, he shook his head. "I don't understand you. You have people here who love you."

Was Logan including himself in those people? "But I also have my career. It's part of who I am. Just like being a cop is part of who you are. Could you quit?"

"That's not the same thing, Meg. You know as well as I do long-distance relationships can't work. Me here. You in Washington and God knows where else."

Avoiding his gaze, she dropped her purse in her lap. "We haven't known each other very long. You can't expect me to make a decision about us because of a few weeks."

"I expect you to make a decision about us because of us."

"Logan, I'm still trying to find my bearings. I—"

"You're running away from people who care about you because you're afraid they'll let you down—like your parents did, like another man did."

She lifted her eyes to his. "So you're a psychologist now?"

"In my line of work, I'm a little bit of everything."

"You think you understand me, but you can't understand your own son. Have I got that right?"

His jaw tensed, and his voice was curt. "That's a low blow, Meg."

She'd never meant to hurt him. But he was hitting hard at her insecurities.

He gathered the remains of their picnic and stuffed them in the bag. "I'll take you home."

Why couldn't he understand her life couldn't revolve around one person? Why couldn't he see the danger in that? "Logan..."

Frowning, he stood. "It's all right, Meg. You call it as you see it. We just don't see it the same way."

He drove her back to Lily and Ned's in silence. They didn't seem to have anything else to say. Meg hurt. She'd been so close to Logan when they'd made love. But now he didn't even want to talk to her. When she climbed out of his car at her aunt's, she didn't know if she'd ever see him again. And she didn't ask because his answer might hurt too much.

Fully expecting to drive to Washington alone Saturday morning, Meg opened her back door and tossed her overnight case inside of her car. Most of her clothes were back at her apartment, so she didn't need much. When she heard tires on the lane, she turned in surprise.

Logan. She hadn't heard from him since the picnic a week ago. After their argument, she presumed he wouldn't want to go with her.

He pulled in beside her car and got out. With each step he took, bringing him closer to her, her heart beat faster.

"My car rides better," he said in a neutral tone.

"I didn't think you'd want to go with me after—"

"I keep my commitments, Meg, even though I make a mess of them sometimes."

His attitude rankled. "This isn't an important one, Logan. If you'd rather not go, you don't have to."

"Meaning I'm easily replaced?"

She was sure she could find an escort among her acquaintances in D.C. Annoyed with his attitude, she responded quickly, "Yes."

His green eyes became hard as his jaw tensed. "Well, I don't want to be replaced, so let's go."

She could tell this was going to be a *fun* trip. But she'd rather have Logan beside her, even when he was pulling his caveman routine than not have him with her.

The ride to D.C. was awkward. Although Logan switched on a soothing radio station, the vibrations inside the car kept Meg from relaxing. As they neared Chevy Chase, she directed him on which exit to take. Her apartment building was easy to find.

The doorman smiled at her. "Welcome back, Miss Dawson. How are you feeling?"

"Pretty good, George. How about you? Is Mary Claire walking yet?"

"Just last week. Now that she's got the ground covered, she's climbin' on everything."

Meg laughed.

Her smile faded as she stepped into the elevator beside Logan and his gaze met hers. She pushed the button for the fourth floor.

Logan remained silent while she unlocked her apartment. Once inside, he asked, "Where do you want the bags?"

She knew what he was asking, and she was tired of pussyfooting around. "Where do *you* want the bags?"

Apparently he was, too. He dropped them on the floor and crossed to her, his face granite hard, his eyes boring into her. "I don't give a damn where we put the bags. But I want to spend the night with you, in your bed. Is that what you want?"

She reached up and stroked his jaw. "Yes."

The tension between them snapped. Logan wrapped his arms around her, and his lips crushed hers. When he broke away, they were both breathless.

He took her face between his palms. "I don't know how to deal with an independent woman."

His admission and the frustration in it made her want to cry and laugh at the same time. "Is that what I am?"

He grimaced. "Unfortunately, yes." Dropping his hands, he paced across the room like a caged tiger. "I'm not used to dealing with a woman like you. You're strong enough to tell me what you want, what you need. Apparently Shelley wasn't. And I have to wonder why. Maybe if I could have let *her* make the decisions, if I hadn't pushed to have more children—"

"Logan, all the what-ifs in the world won't change the past. You're a strong man. I imagine you've always known what you want."

He shook his head and faced her. "That's no excuse for not listening. Maybe you were right. Maybe I don't know my own son because I don't really listen to him, either."

Meg crossed to Logan and wrapped her arms around him in a hug. He stood rigid, as if he didn't know how to accept the comfort. Finally he enfolded her in his arms.

She twined hers around his neck and stroked his nape. "You can start listening anytime."

"Not when you're doing that," he growled, and swept her into his arms.

Since Meg only had one bedroom, finding it wasn't a problem. Logan lowered her to the bed and opened the top button on her blouse. "This time we're going to take it slow." When he finished with her blouse, he went to push it from her shoulders.

She caught his hand to stop him.

"What's wrong?"

"The last time I...wasn't completely undressed. My shoulder...it's not pretty."

He lifted her chin and rubbed his thumb over the point. "Everything about you is pretty. Sit up so we can take this off."

Meg sat up and pulled her blouse from her jeans. Logan helped push it from her shoulders. For a long moment, he studied the red lines. Then he leaned toward her and, with incomparable gentleness, kissed each line, each scar, until she knew they truly didn't matter to him.

Logan helped strip off Meg's clothes slowly, kissing her arms, her fingertips and, a few moments later, her knees and calves. Each piece of clothing melted away under the firmness and heat of his lips, the stroking eroticism of his fingertips.

When she was naked before him, quivering from his kisses and caresses, she said, "Now it's your turn."

His brows arched as he smiled. "And that means?"

She sat up and pulled his shirt free of his jeans. "That there are advantages to keeping company with an independent woman." After the first button, she kissed his chest. After the third, she splayed the plackets open and rubbed her fingertips over a dark nipple.

He shuddered.

Smiling, she unbuttoned the rest and placed a slow, wet kiss above his navel.

"Meg. What are you trying to do?"

Her hands worked his belt while she looked up and teased, "Didn't you say you wanted to do this slowly?"

The green of his eyes deepened with the desire evident in his taut muscles, his husky voice. "I never realized it would be such torture."

When she answered Logan by cupping him, he groaned and took her by the hands. "That's it." He stripped, took foil packets from his pocket and lay beside her on the bed. Then he dropped the packets on the nightstand.

They gazed at each other, absorbing the other's presence, just relishing the moment. Meg brushed her hand over his shoulder. "I was afraid I'd never see you again."

"It crossed my mind," he said honestly. "Especially when you didn't call."

"When *I* didn't call?" She withdrew her hand.

He caught it and brought it to his lips. Gently, with a sexy grin, he nibbled and kissed her palm until she sighed. "The more I thought about *not* seeing you again, the more restless I got. Then I started thinking about my history with women and your history. You needed your independence to survive emotionally, and you have every right to make decisions you feel are right for you. I might not agree, but that's my problem. Too often I forced my opinions on Shelley. Or else she just wasn't confident enough to stand up for what she believed."

Meg tried to keep herself free of the sensual haze Logan induced and paid attention to his words. She knew they were important. "It sounds as if you've done a lot of thinking."

"I have. And it all boils down to the fact that I'm not ready to give you up." Leaning toward her, he kissed her tenderly, letting the passion build.

With soft words and feverish caresses, he kissed and touched her everywhere until she was trembling from head to toe, needing him in the most elemental way. But this time she wanted to touch him, too. His back was smooth to his waist, where she discovered a few silky hairs. Every inch of him was strong and muscular and hot. And when she stroked his thigh higher and higher until she curled her fingers around him, she knew she'd found an intimacy with Logan of which she'd been afraid to dream. She could feel the beat of his pulse in her hand, and when she stroked him, he made a deep sound in his throat and closed her tight in his arms. She'd never felt more safe or more cherished. If only the feeling could last forever.

But Logan had other feelings in mind. Drawing her on top of him, he entered her slowly. Then he let her set the pace. Tears came to her eyes. He was telling her she was his equal and that they could share their passion, not compete, not make promises they couldn't keep. He held her waist, kept his eyes on hers and joined her in their ascent up the mountain.

Just when Meg thought she'd reached the top and could grasp the pleasure and hold on to it, it exploded all around her, shaking her and frightening her. Because the moment before the ecstasy overtook her, she realized the deepest truth of all—she loved Logan. Heaven help her, she loved him. The realization scared her to death, because if she loved him, she'd have to trust him. She wasn't sure she could trust anyone.

After Todd, she'd promised herself, no matter whom she met or what situation she got herself into, she would only trust herself. But trust went with love, didn't it? Yet how did independence and trust fit together?

As she leaned forward, laying her cheek on Logan's shoulder, feeling his heart beating, she realized she was more frightened than she'd ever been. In Costa Rica her life had been in danger, but here...now...her heart was on the line. Did she have the courage to give it to Logan and trust him to keep it safe?

Chapter Eleven

A waiter offered Logan a glass of champagne from a silver tray, but he declined, keeping his gaze on Meg. Ever since they'd walked into the ballroom, one person after another had greeted her. Mostly men. What man wouldn't look at her in that dress? It was emerald green and molded to her much too well from her breasts to her ankles. The slit halfway up her thigh made it sexy as sin.

To be fair, the men looked at her, all right, but they talked to her, too. She was obviously well respected. And here she was in her element. She glittered and glowed, more than the gold earrings swinging on her ears. For all his talk of accepting her independence and the decisions she made, he regretted how well she seemed to thrive in this atmosphere. He was hoping she'd return to D.C., see the emptiness of it and want to spend the rest of her days in Willow Valley. That was a foolish pipe dream on his part.

After they'd made love this afternoon, she'd changed, becoming quiet and distant. He'd asked her if anything was wrong. She'd just smiled and said, "No." But there was something in her eyes. If he didn't know better, he'd think it was fear.

She'd been talking to the same guy for fifteen minutes. Suddenly her gaze connected with Logan's. After another minute or so, she walked toward him. Once she was beside him, she asked, "Are you bored?"

"I can think of other things I'd rather be doing," he drawled.

She smiled coyly. "Walking on the mall?"

"We did that this afternoon."

Tilting her head she offered, "I'd suggest visiting the Smithsonian, but it's closed."

"Not quite what I had in mind, either." He stuffed one hand into his trouser pocket. "Who was that guy?"

She looked toward the man who had engaged her in conversation. "He's a journalist."

"Known him for long?" Logan asked, unable to keep the edge from his voice.

"About five years." She studied him for a long moment. "Logan, are you jealous?"

"Hell, yes, I'm jealous. You're my lady now, and I don't particularly relish watching while other men undress you with their eyes."

He thought she might get her hackles up. But instead of getting angry, she laid her hand on his arm and said, "But I only let *you* undress me."

The husky desire in her voice, the sincerity in her wide brown eyes, aroused him. He tapped one of her dangling gold earrings. "Do you intend to mingle much longer?"

"Not if you'd rather go back to my apartment."

"You're certain?"

"I'm positive."

Meg was so unlike Shelley—so sure of herself, what she had to do, what she needed. "Then let's go, pretty lady. Because right now there's no place else I'd rather be."

Back at the apartment, Logan took off his tuxedo jacket and tossed it over a chair. Meg's apartment, even at night, was very much like her. Flowers and vines in rose and green on white covered her love seat and chair. The wicker tables added lightness to the small area. The kitchen was painted yellow and white with touches of green here and there. *Vibrant, warm* and *alive* were words that came to Logan's mind.

After making sure all locks were in place, he went to Meg's bedroom. It was simple but elegant—an off-white spread, ruffled curtains that crisscrossed the windows. Meg stood at the dresser removing her earrings. She smiled at him in the mirror.

He came up behind her and wrapped his arms around her. "How would you like to go hiking next Saturday with me and Travis?"

"Maybe the two of you should go alone."

His eyes stayed on hers. "I'm afraid he won't go if it's just the two of us. He seems to like you."

"So you want to use me as a buffer."

Logan dropped his arms and stepped back. "I can understand if you'd rather not go."

When she turned to face him, her voice was gentle. "I didn't say that. I just don't want Travis to think I'm invading his territory."

He should have known Meg would think about Travis, too. "All right. I'll ask him if he wants you to come along. Maybe it'll get some honest conversation going between us."

"And you'll tell me the truth about what he says."

Logan nodded. "Always." He ran his fingers along the edge of her dress above her breasts. "Do you need help getting out of this?"

Slipping her arms around his waist, she unlatched his cummerbund. "If you need help getting out of this."

Logan lifted her off the floor, bringing her lips to his. His answer was in his kiss.

Meg's restlessness woke Logan. She tossed from side to side. When beads of perspiration dotted her forehead and she said, "No, no. Don't shoot!" Logan knew she was having a nightmare rather than a dream.

He clasped her arm. "Meg. Wake up. It's only a dream."

Not hearing him, she clutched her shoulder and moaned. She was shaking all over.

Quickly he slipped his arm around her. "C'mon, sweetheart, wake up. Meg. Wake up."

Her eyes fluttered open.

Logan stroked her tears away. "It was a bad dream. You're awake now."

Recognition dawned in her eyes.

"Do you want to talk about it?"

She shook her head, and her lower lip quivered. "Would you just hold me?"

Wrapping his arms around her, he settled her against his chest. After they'd made love, they'd fallen asleep in each other's arms. With Meg tucked against his shoulder, Logan had fallen asleep easily. But holding her then and holding her now were two different things. She trembled against him, but not from desire. The kidnapping still haunted her. Suddenly he realized her decision to return to work might be something she had to do for her emotional survival.

A week later, Meg glanced at the darkening sky, hoping the expedition Logan had planned wasn't a mistake. The hiking trail wove through wooded terrain like a thin ribbon. As the incline became steeper, it was only wide enough for one person at a time. Meg glanced at the sky again. The day had started out sunny. They'd been hiking about an hour when the sun had disappeared behind a cloud.

Logan trudged along first. Meg followed, with Travis bringing up the rear. He'd been sullen throughout the morning, and Meg wondered if Logan had bribed him to come today. Maybe she could get father and son talking to one another when they ate lunch.

Stopping for a moment, Meg looked over her shoulder. Travis hiked about twenty feet behind her. "Are you getting hungry?"

He gave her a very slight smile. "I'm *always* hungry."

At least he talked to her in more than monosyllabic sentences. Maybe if she could *keep* him talking... "I packed liverwurst."

"You what?"

She grinned. "Just kidding. Ham and cheese and turkey and cheese."

They trekked on in silence a few more minutes. Suddenly she sensed he was right behind her.

"I talked to Mr. Holden about the exchange program."

She moved to the side to make room for him on the trail. "And?"

"He said if I keep my grades up, it's a possibility second semester next year."

She clapped him on the shoulder. "That's terrific."

"I was wondering..." He seemed hesitant to continue.

"What were you wondering?"

"Well, this is my third year of Spanish. But like you said, school learning's not the same as actually speaking it with someone. I wondered if while you're in Willow Valley, you and me could practice. If you have some spare time. I heard you telling Dad about working at the adoption service. If you're too busy, I understand."

"For now I'm only working there in the mornings. I want to make sure Aunt Lily doesn't overdo. But if you want to stop by after school a couple of days a week, that would be fine."

"You mean it?"

She saw the doubts in Travis's eyes. "Yes, I mean it."

"Because of Dad?"

Travis was trying so hard to assert his independence. She understood what he was asking her. She laid her hand on his arm. "Your dad and I are seeing each other now. You know that, right?"

"Yeah. I knew Dad was going to Washington with you."

"No matter what does or doesn't happen with me and your dad, you and I can still be friends. Got it?"

He grinned, a real full-fledged grin. "Got it. Is Monday afternoon okay?"

"Monday's fine."

The path narrowed even more, and Travis dropped back again.

A short while later, Logan stopped before a sharp rise and waited for Meg to catch up. "How are you doing?"

They'd managed little time alone since the past weekend. Wednesday night, they'd stolen an hour away in Lily and Ned's barn. Afterward, laughing, they'd brushed the hay from each other's hair. Remembering, she smiled. "I'm fine."

He offered her water from the bottle hanging on his belt. After popping the lid, he held the water out to her. When she took it from him, his fingers purposefully slid over hers, telling her he wanted to touch her more. She took a few swallows and handed it back to him. He sipped from the spot her lips had touched.

Meg wondered if the bond growing between her and Logan was making matters worse instead of better for him and his son as Travis came up to them and frowned.

Logan reattached the bottle to his belt. "Once we climb this hill, we can stop and eat."

Travis shrugged. "Whatever. I just want to get back. I have plans to meet Kyle at the Pizza Shop for supper."

Meg could tell Logan was counting to ten. As Travis started off in front of them, he said, "No progress so far."

"The day's only half-over," she soothed.

He slid his hand under her hair and stroked her neck. "Always an optimist."

Closing her eyes, she relished the feel of his fingers and wondered why she loved his touch so. Maybe because she loved him. She was getting used to the idea . . . slowly.

By the time they'd finished lunch, Meg felt like tearing her hair out strand by strand. Travis met Logan's attempts at conversation, as well as hers, with brooding silence. She was about ready to take Travis by his ears and shake him, and she realized this was probably how frustrated Logan felt on a daily basis.

When they took to the trail again, she guessed all three of them had a common goal—get the day over with. As they hiked up a steeper, rocky incline, her mind sorted through all the possibilities of things she could say to get through to Travis. Thinking about taking him aside for a heart-to-heart when they returned, she wasn't as careful as she should have been on the path. She lost her footing.

One minute she was upright; the next she'd let out a yelp and was sliding down the packed earth on her bottom.

Travis got to her first and slid his arm around her shoulders to help her sit up. "Take a deep breath if you can. You probably got the wind knocked out of you."

Logan appeared by her side seconds later and snapped, "Don't move her until I find out if she's all right." He took her hand and gentled his voice. "Does anything hurt?"

Travis's arm was still supporting her shoulders, but it was rigid with tension.

She sat up on her own, moved her arms and legs and took a few breaths. Her right forearm was sore, and she realized she'd scrapped it on the slide downward. "I'm fine. Tomorrow might be a different story."

Logan directed, "Bend your arms and legs."

She did, and winced when she bent her arm.

"Let's take a look." He unbuttoned her cuff and rolled up her sleeve. She'd scraped the skin.

Travis shifted his backpack from his shoulders. "I have a first-aid kit." Quickly he found it and opened it. After taking out a small plastic bottle of peroxide, he unscrewed the lid.

Logan took a cotton patch from the little box and took the peroxide from Travis. "I'll do it."

Travis slapped the box on the ground. "Fine. You do it. Like you do everything!"

"Travis. Watch your mouth."

"What are you going to do if I don't? Oh, I know. Send me to military school. Well, that couldn't be any worse than living with you. You don't want me there, any more than you want me here today. Anybody can see you two'd rather be in bed together."

"You apologize to Meg. Now." Logan's expression was so fierce, Meg was afraid he'd slap his son.

"Do I have to apologize to you, too? What for? Telling the truth?"

The two males stared each other down until Meg couldn't stand it anymore. "Will you two please *talk* to each other?" When only silence met her question, she asked the teenager, "Why do you think your dad doesn't want you around?"

Travis pushed himself to his feet. "He just doesn't. I *know* it." He looked at the hill and said, "I'll meet you at the top."

After he scrambled off, Meg said to Logan, "Go after him. Talk to him."

"He won't listen to me, Meg."

"You're not listening to each other!"

Thunder rumbled, and they both looked up at the darkening sky. Logan poured peroxide onto the cotton patch. "Let's get you fixed up and home. If you soak in a hot tub tonight, you might not feel so sore tomorrow."

Meg was ready to bop both MacDonald males over the head with something heavy. They were more alike than they knew.

Lightning flashed, and drops of rain began to fall. Logan had been keeping a sharp eye on Meg as Travis led their trek. She seemed fine, but he wanted to make sure she wasn't hiding an injury so he wouldn't worry.

The rain fell in earnest, and Logan called to his son, "Travis, hold up."

Logan untied his jacket from around his waist. When he caught up to Meg, he put it around her shoulders. "This will keep you drier than your sweater."

"Travis, I said hold up," Logan repeated as his son kept walking.

Travis called over his shoulder, "The only way we're going to get back is to keep going."

Logan ran up ahead and caught his son by his arm. "I said stop."

"I don't want to stop. I told you I have plans."

"I'm not going to let us get soaking wet because you have plans. There's a lean-to around the next bend. We'll wait it out there."

Lightning shot through the sky, and the blast of thunder followed.

A few minutes later, the three of them sat on the floor of the lean-to while the rain came down steadily on the roof. Travis had wound his arms around his long legs and rested his chin on his knees.

Logan wished he could get through to him. He wished... "What are you and Kyle going to do tonight?"

"Nothing illegal," Travis answered sarcastically.

"When I ask a civil question, I expect a civil answer."

Travis lifted his head and stretched out his legs. "I'm not a suspect, Dad. So leave me alone."

Anger and pain beat in Logan's chest. "I will not leave you alone. You're my *son!*"

"And you wish I wasn't."

Travis's statement hit Logan between the eyes. "What?"

"You heard me," Travis mumbled, looking at his sneakers.

"Where did you get an idea like that?" Logan asked, wishing he could read his son's mind.

"From you."

Logan reached out and grabbed Travis's arm. "You can't believe that. What did I ever do or say to make you think it?"

Travis hesitated a second, then murmured, "Plenty."

He tried to pull away, but Logan wouldn't let him. "Tell me, Travis. Tell me what's going on with you. I've asked you before, and now I want the truth. Why did you run away?"

"Your rules and regulations, curfews—"

Smoke and mirrors—the same thing he thought they'd been fighting about for four years. "The truth, Travis."

Travis wrenched away, and his green eyes smacked into Logan's. "All right. You want the truth. I'll tell you the truth. You never loved Mom. And you never wanted me. I heard you fighting that night. I'd come home from a game and was standing on the deck. If you didn't love her, you shouldn't have married her! You shouldn't have had me!" With that, Travis jumped up and ran from the lean-to into the pouring rain.

Logan put his hand on Meg's knee. "I have to go after him."

She nodded. "Of course you do. Go."

Logan found Travis running along the path. He clasped his son's elbow. "You're wrong. I have *always* wanted you. I married your mother *because of you.*"

"You shouldn't have. Not if you didn't love her. The two of you should have just gotten rid of me."

"No!" Logan shouted to Travis and the world as rain dripped from his face. "I didn't love your mother as I should have. But I was committed to her, committed to you, committed to our life as a family. My mistake was trying to convince your mother to want the same things I did."

"What things?" Travis clenched his hands at his sides.

Logan had always tried to protect his son. Maybe it was time to stop. "More children, for one. I thought when we moved to Willow Valley, we could revitalize our marriage. I thought we'd try to have more children. But your mom and I didn't agree. We argued about it that night and she ran out. Don't you think I blame myself for her death as much as you blame me?'' The guilt and anguish Logan had felt over Shelley's accident poured over him with the rain.

The question hung between him and his son as the drops pelted down.

''You do blame me, don't you?'' he pressed, knowing if he and Travis were going to have a relationship, it had to be based on honesty.

''It's your fault she ran out. Every time I miss her . . .'' Travis's voice broke.

''You blame me,'' Logan finished.

Thunder rolled. Travis's eyes flashed defiance. ''Yes.''

His son was breaking his heart. But he deserved it. Somehow he had to make peace with it so they could both go on. ''I can't fault you for that. And I can't be angry with you because of it. But I am angry with myself because I didn't know what was going on in your head. Travis, no one is as important to me as you. Can you believe me?''

''I dunno,'' he mumbled.

''I have always wanted you. From the moment your mother told me she was pregnant.''

Travis raised his chin and, as the rain dripped down his face, he asked, ''What about Mom?''

Logan couldn't tell Travis the truth about that. Besides, eventually Shelley did want and love their son. ''You know your mom loved you.''

Travis searched Logan's face. After a while, he said, ''Yeah, she did. But that night, why did she say she shouldn't have married you?''

"Because she didn't want to get married. I talked her into it. I thought we'd be happy. I thought I could make her happy. But I couldn't."

"Is that why she said you ruined her life?"

"Travis..."

"Dad, tell me the truth," Travis pleaded, his green eyes large and deep and hurting.

Logan couldn't ignore his son's plea. "Yes."

Comprehension dawned in Travis's eyes. "*She* didn't want me."

His son's pain was Logan's, too. "Only at first. She was younger than I was. She found out she was pregnant and panicked. But she did love you, Travis."

"*You* made her keep me."

Logan took his son by the shoulders. "I convinced her to marry me. That might have been a mistake. But keeping you and having you was not a mistake. The problems were between me and your mother."

Travis looked confused. "Do you miss her?"

"Yes, I miss her. And I ache because she died the way she did. It shouldn't have happened." More than anything, Logan wanted to hug Travis. But there was still a wall around the boy that he wouldn't let his father penetrate. They stood there for what seemed like hours, letting the storm swirl around them.

The rain plastered Logan's shirt to his body, and Travis was just as wet. Finally Logan said, "We're soaked. And Meg's probably worried. Let's go back."

Travis looked toward the lean-to, then nodded. They walked back together, not touching and not speaking, but Logan felt they'd opened a window. Maybe now some air and sun could get in. If not today... maybe soon.

When Meg spotted them, her eyes widened but she didn't scold. Rather, she shrugged out of Logan's jacket, then stripped off her pullover sweater, leaving only her cotton blouse.

"You'll get cold," Logan chided.

"And you two will catch pneumonia if you don't get out of at least some of those wet clothes. I know you're both stubborn, but believe me, I can be just as stubborn."

Logan checked his son's face.

Meg handed the jacket to Logan. "Shirt off, jacket on. No arguments."

He knew Travis might follow his lead. "You're tough," he grumbled.

"You don't know the half of it," she responded, holding the sweater out to Travis. "The same goes for you."

Logan's confrontation with Travis had left him shaken but hopeful. Maybe with everything out in the open, they could start fresh. Trying to establish a connection between them, he asked, "Do you think we should make her turn around?"

Travis shrugged, and then his lips turned up in a small smile. "She *could* close her eyes, though."

With an exaggerated but patient sigh, Meg did.

Mighty rolls of thunder continued to echo through the lean-to. Lightning cracked close by. None of it seemed to faze Meg. Logan knew Shelley would have cowered close to his side. Yet he remembered Meg waking up from her nightmare, asking him to hold her. She was strong but vulnerable, and he felt more for her each day. How would his relationship with Meg affect his son? Of course, if Meg didn't stay...

As they sat munching on trail mix in a stilted silence, Meg asked, "Have you discovered anything more on the break-in at the high school?"

Logan knew she was trying to make conversation to cover the awkwardness. "Dead ends every way we look. No gossip. The kids aren't talking."

"The kids don't know anything," Travis mumbled.

"How do you know?" Logan asked. After all, Travis was on the scene, in the midst of it.

His son shrugged again. "I don't for sure. But the school's not that big. Even if someone's covering for somebody else, they usually slip. Nothing is going around. Zilch."

Logan frowned. "That means either someone outside the school did it or else someone in the school is intending to do it again."

"How do you figure?" Travis asked.

"If it was a prank, someone would know something because there's pride in carrying it off. Whoever did it must need the money."

Travis looked thoughtful. "When I was on the streets, no one told anyone anything. It was too risky. You didn't even tell where you were going to crash that night."

"Where did you crash, Travis?" Logan had tried before, unsuccessfully, to get his son to talk about his experience.

Travis looked defiant for a moment, but then the defiance faded. "Wherever I could. Garages. You wouldn't believe how many people use 'em for storage instead of their cars. Factory warehouses. Security is lousy on most of them."

"Travis, did you ever get hurt other than the mugging?" Meg's caring voice was a request for information rather than a judgment.

Logan waited for the answer, every muscle in his body tense. It was the question he'd wanted to ask ever since Travis had come home.

Although Meg had asked the question, Travis directed his answer to his father. "No. I got a few bumps and bruises now and then when someone tried to steal my stuff, but I never got hurt. Not till the mugging."

Logan let out his pent-up breath. "Thank God."

Meg took his hand, and Travis saw it. But he didn't comment.

A short time later, the rain let up. Logan watched Meg carefully as he let Travis lead and he followed Meg. The wet rocks and mud made the going slower than usual. Every fifteen minutes or so, Travis checked behind him to make sure he wasn't getting too far ahead.

Logan had time to think as they hiked. The full impact of Travis's misconceptions hit him. He couldn't believe that for four years, his son had believed that not only was Logan responsible for Shelley's death, but that he'd never wanted a child to begin with. No wonder Travis's behavior had been such a trial. No wonder he held such hostility. Logan had compounded the problem by cracking down harder, thinking more discipline had been the answer.

What kind of a father knew so little about his child that he couldn't see the signs, that he wasn't intuitive enough to get to the bottom of the problem? Travis had a right to be angry, resentful and distant. They'd lost so much ground. Logan wasn't sure they'd ever be able to recover. Now that he knew the root of the problem, he still didn't have the answers. All he could do was try to be as open and honest with his son as he could, and hope Travis would do the same.

He couldn't help asking himself if he and Shelley should have divorced. Would she be alive today if they had? The guilt for coaxing her into marriage sometimes seemed like a ten-ton weight. All those years, there had been a separateness between them, a tension that he thought they'd hidden but obviously not well enough. Travis had felt it on some level. That's why now he believed so easily that he'd been a mistake, that they'd never really wanted him.

As Logan, Meg and Travis arrived at the area where Logan had parked the car, they were quiet. He guessed Meg just wanted to soak in a hot tub. His own jeans were wet and uncomfortable, and he figured Travis itched to get home, get changed and go meet Kyle. The silence lasted as they climbed into the car and Logan drove down the winding road that led out of the trail area. They'd only traveled about a quarter of a mile when Logan spotted the felled tree blocking the narrow road.

He stopped and considered their options. Opening his door, he said, "I'm going to take a look."

A few minutes later, Travis and Meg stood beside him. Thinking about the way he'd handled his son over the years, instead of making a unilateral decision Logan asked, "What do you think?"

The teenager looked surprised that Logan wanted his opinion. He shrugged. "We might be able to move it."

Logan smiled. "If we're lucky, it's hollow."

"No such luck," Travis mumbled as he gave the trunk a shove with his foot.

"What can I do?" Meg asked.

"Get back in the car and relax. Travis and I will see what we can do."

When she hesitated, Travis encouraged her. "Go on. Dad and I will take care of this."

Relieved her help wasn't needed, relieved the two MacDonald men seemed to want to work together instead of backing away from each other, she settled in the front seat and laid her head against the headrest. A wave of nausea washed over her. She was tired. So tired.

The nausea subsided. This had been an emotional day. More so for Logan and Travis, but she'd felt caught in the midst of it. She didn't know what the two MacDonalds had said to each other out in the rain, but something was different—especially the way they looked at each other. Now they seemed to *see* each other.

For Logan's sake, as well as Travis's, she hoped they could find some common ground.

Fighting her fatigue, she lifted her head and watched. Travis and Logan used a long branch as a lever, then rolled and pushed the tree trunk back far enough that the car could fit through. When they returned to the car, they wore satisfied expressions, as if they'd accomplished something.

Logan drove Meg to Lily and Ned's. As he braked, Meg rested her hand on his arm. "You don't have to get out. You two need hot showers as much as I need a hot bath."

But Logan wouldn't let her go that easily. Surprising her, he leaned close and gave her a quick kiss. "I'll call you."

With a peek at Travis, she realized he looked pensive rather than defiant. She hopped out of the car and told them both goodbye. Maybe Travis would stay home tonight and talk with Logan. Maybe they would begin to realize they were more alike than different.

Meg insisted on cleaning up after supper so Lily and Ned could take an evening stroll. The sky had cleared, becoming pale blue before the sun set. Finally, when she'd clicked on the dishwasher and headed upstairs, she realized her right hip was as sore as her arm. As she soaked in the tub, she almost fell asleep. The sounds of her aunt and uncle returning from their walk urged her to leave the now-lukewarm water.

She'd wrapped herself in her robe and was drying her hair when her aunt opened the bathroom door. "I'm perturbed with you, young lady. Logan's on the phone. He told me you took a spill today."

"I'm fine, Aunt Lily. I slipped. That's all." She hadn't wanted to give her aunt anything to worry about. Although Lily was recovering nicely and had resumed many of her activities, the doctor had told her to try to keep stress to a minimum.

"You should have let *me* clean up the kitchen," her aunt chided.

"*You* made supper," Meg argued.

"I stuck a chicken in the oven with a few vegetables." Lily looked her over. "Are you sure you're okay? You looked pale at supper."

Meg slipped by the woman who loved her like a mother. "Don't worry. A good night's sleep is all I need." A few moments later, she picked up the phone in her room. "Logan MacDonald. Why did you tell Aunt Lily about my fall?"

"I merely asked how you felt. I didn't know if you'd tell me."

"Why wouldn't I?"

"Because you think you can handle everything yourself."

She sighed. "I think you know me a little too well."

"Not nearly well enough," he responded in a deep, sexy voice that almost made her forget her fatigue. Knowing they couldn't spend the night together but longing to cuddle in his arms, she asked, "How are you and Travis?"

He allowed the change of subject. "I'm not sure. We're both watching what we say and how we say it. But something happened out there today, Meg. Even though it hurt like hell, we got the raw truth out in the open. Now all I have to do is make him believe that he's important to me and always has been. He thought Shelley and I never wanted him, that it would have been better if he hadn't been born."

She could hear the pain and regret in Logan's voice. "He'll believe you. Just take it slowly."

"I've had sixteen years and suddenly I feel as if I'm starting from square one."

"You are. But he'll come around."

"You've made a difference."

"Logan . . ."

"You have. You were right. I needed to see his point of view. After today, I think I can." Following a pause, Logan asked, "You know what I'd like to do this very moment?"

"What?"

"Make love to you."

There was almost too much desire in his words, too much feeling in her heart. Fear tapped her on the shoulder again. Closing her eyes, she tried to will it away. When she couldn't, she pretended a lightness she didn't feel. "In the barn?"

"Anywhere at all."

With a shiver of passion attached to the love flowing through her, she took a deep breath, realizing that leaving Willow Valley would be even more difficult than standing on her aunt's porch when she was twelve and watching her parents drive away.

When Meg raised her arm to knock softly on Victoria Lee's office door Monday afternoon, the sleeve of her blouse brushed her scrape, and she winced. Then she ignored the soreness as she had all morning. It would heal.

"Come in."

Meg stepped inside. "I spoke with our contact in Guatemala. Everything is finalized on the Conlin adoption. They leave tomorrow and pick up the baby on Wednesday. They're ecstatic."

"They've waited two years to adopt."

Handing the file to Victoria, Meg said, "Mrs. Conlin was crying. Did you know she and her husband went through procedures for five years, and none of the surgeries or fertility drugs worked? For seven years, she and her husband have prayed for this child."

Victoria laid the manila folder on her desk. "I know. A lot of our couples have a similar history." She gestured to the chair in front of her desk. When Meg was seated, she asked, "You're enjoying your work with the agency, aren't you?"

Meg was beginning to love her work here. The past week, she'd thought more and more about staying in

Willow Valley. Logan was becoming part of every fiber of her life, as well as her being. If she enjoyed helping couples adopt, if she gave in to her feelings for Logan, the nightmares would disappear. Wouldn't they? She felt safe when Logan held her. Her love for him grew each day. But she hadn't told him yet. It was so soon. So new.

"I *do* enjoy my work here."

"The liaison position is still open. I've held off interviewing anyone else, hoping you'd change your mind and accept my offer."

Meg brushed her hair from her cheek. "I can't make the decision yet. I'm sorry."

Victoria leaned back in her chair. "I'm going to take the chance that placing babies with loving couples will be more valuable work to you than any you've experienced. So I'm going to give you until Christmas to decide. Fair enough?"

Meg thought about Logan and smiled. With a joyful feeling in her heart, she agreed, "Fair enough."

Chapter Twelve

The sun peeked over the horizon, casting the earliest rays of daylight onto the barn. Meg sat in her bedroom Thanksgiving morning, staring into the backyard. She'd been awake most of the night. She had to pull herself together, she had to stuff the turkey, she had to...

She had to talk to Logan.

Her life had never been more complicated, and there were no simple answers. Would Logan be angry? Upset?

Meg placed her hand on her stomach, sensing the life there, loving it, knowing for certain she'd never abandon this child, call it a mistake or give it any reason to believe it wasn't important, valued, loved. She would never call this child an accident, although the first time was the only time she and Logan hadn't used birth control. What was the phrase? *Love child.* She loved Logan and she'd love this child.

She didn't know if Logan loved her. He desired her, but passion was not love.

A month had passed since their hike. She'd missed the signs of pregnancy at first—fatigue, the late-afternoon nausea, a missed period—blaming all of it on the trauma of being kidnapped and wounded. Enjoying her time with Logan, whether they talked or stole away to make love, she'd gotten caught up with being in love. Until the day before yesterday, when supper had been a chore to eat and she'd lost it soon afterward. She'd made an appointment with Doc Jacobs. He'd put the symptoms together immediately, taken a blood sample and given her the results. She was pregnant.

Lily had invited Travis and Logan to Thanksgiving dinner. Meg had looked forward to this day. But now part of her wished she could go back to bed, pull the covers over her head and not get up again until she knew exactly what to do about everything—her career, possibly accepting a position with the adoption agency, but, most of all, Logan.

Meg wouldn't let Lily do anything except mash potatoes. It was difficult keeping her aunt in line. Yesterday, when Meg had returned from Doc Jacobs's, she found Lily taking two pumpkin pies from the oven. So Meg had made her aunt promise to behave today. Except Meg's idea of behaving and her aunt's were entirely different.

Finally, when Logan and Travis arrived in the early evening, Lily let them take her place in the kitchen.

Logan came to Meg as she put the finishing touches on a salad, put his arms around her and kissed her on the neck. "Happy Thanksgiving."

His touch, his voice and the knowledge she now carried brought tears to her eyes. She swallowed hard and managed to reply, "Happy Thanksgiving."

Travis pulled out a chair and sat at the table already set with Lily's best china. "Are you two going to cook or make out? Some of us are getting hungry."

When Meg turned around, she saw Travis's grin. She'd seen a change in him over the past month. His hostility had given way to an honest friendliness to her and a more accepting attitude of his father. Over the past few weeks, she'd seen Logan relax more with his son. They still didn't talk much, but when they did, they seemed to be more willing to listen to each other.

She couldn't help but think of the child she was carrying. How would Logan relate to him or her? Did he want to be a father again? And if not...

Travis's grin faded, and he was looking at her as if wondering if he'd said something wrong.

Summoning up a smile, she responded, "We're almost finished cooking. If one of you strong men would like to lift the bird out of the oven—"

The phone rang, and Meg reached for it. "Hello."

"Meg, darling, it's your mother. We just got back to the village and received your messages about Lily. It sounds as if the crisis is over."

When Meg had tried to reach her parents after Lily's heart attack, she'd been told they'd left for an archaeological dig. She'd called their base site each week, leaving a message with an update of her aunt's condition so they'd have it when they returned. Old sadness surfaced when she heard her mother's voice. But anger soon followed. Anger like she'd never known.

Even when they'd learned of Meg's ordeal and injury, they'd made two solicitous phone calls, discovered she'd recover and gone back to their work. She found herself angry not only for herself but for her aunt. "Yes, the crisis is over. For now. What I'd like to know is how you would have felt if she'd died and you were just calling in now?"

"Margaret Elizabeth. How dare you speak to me like that?"

"I dare because it's the truth. Would you like to speak to Aunt Lily?"

"Yes, of course. But first, how are you?"

Pregnant, Mother. And believe me, you'll be the last to know. "I'm terrific."

"Good. Good. I just wanted you to know we'll be back in the States in about a month. It's time to raise funds again, so we'll be doing a tour of colleges and private companies."

"Are you and Dad well?" As much as she didn't want to, she still loved her parents and cared about their welfare.

"Yes, of course."

Silence extended between them. They had no more to say. "I'll get Aunt Lily. Hold on."

When Meg returned to the kitchen, she listened to make sure her aunt had picked up, then replaced the phone on its cradle. Logan and Travis were looking at her as if she'd grown two heads. She opened the oven door and pulled out the rack.

Logan crossed to the stove. "I'll get it."

She stood back and let him lift it to the top of the range.

He lifted off the lid and asked casually, "That was your mother?"

"Yes. They'll be coming back to the States around Christmas."

Travis stood and joined her by the sink. "You don't sound too happy about it."

Whether it was hormones or the tension she felt because of the news she had to give Logan, she just wanted to cry. "I'm not happy or unhappy about it. What they do no longer affects me."

"You can't mean that," Logan chided.

"I know exactly what I mean and how I feel." She faced Travis. "If you want to see an example of parents who really *don't* care, just drop by when they're here."

Logan and his son exchanged a look that said they didn't know what had gotten into her. She wasn't entirely sure herself. But she did know she loved her baby already, and her protective instincts had revved into overdrive from the moment she'd heard her mother's voice. She would never, ever hurt her child as her parents had hurt her. She would never abandon her son or daughter.

This tension was driving her crazy, that's all. As soon as they finished dinner, she'd tell Logan about the baby.

Lily and Ned loved having more people in their house for the holiday. Conversation flowed around the table as Meg struggled to keep her mind on it and answer questions when someone addressed her directly. Every once in a while, she caught Logan's gaze on her.

She pushed her food around her plate, managing a bite or two.

After dinner, Travis left to join friends. Lily and Ned insisted on helping Logan and Meg with cleanup, though Meg would have preferred to work with Logan and ease into the conversation they needed to have. Finally Meg washed the roasting pan and sighed with relief as Ned and Lily went to the living room.

Logan quickly dried the pan. "Do you feel like getting some fresh air?"

Meg jumped at the chance. "I'll get my jacket."

A few minutes later, they walked along the path in the backyard. A whippoorwill sang into the night. The stars, brilliant against the black sky, twinkled through the bare branches. So many changes in the past month. She could already feel the changes in her body, now that she was aware of what was happening.

"What's wrong, Meg?" Logan's tone was gentle, but also held that determination that was innately his to cut to the bottom line.

Stopping, she faced him, not knowing how to say it the best way. "I'm pregnant."

Silence. The light from the back porch reached only far enough to cast shadows, but she could see Logan's jaw tense. Finally, as hours seemed to pass, she heard him blow out a breath.

"Say it," she said.

Still, he remained silent.

"Go ahead, Logan. Tell me how you feel . . . as if you're in the middle of history repeating itself."

"How do you feel?" he asked without responding to her statement.

She wasn't sure what she expected, but this wasn't it. Had she expected Logan to suddenly declare his undying love? Maybe she hadn't expected it, but searching her heart, she had to admit that had been a hope. "I'm confused and scared. I just found out yesterday, so it hasn't had time to sink in."

"You don't have to go through it alone." There was sincerity in his voice, but distance, too.

Any hope she'd entertained about happily-ever-after wilted. She should have known better. She should have known she couldn't count on anyone but herself. Despite Logan's halfhearted promise of support, she knew she had to make decisions that were more than convenient—they had to be right for her and her baby. She'd never depended on anyone; she wasn't about to start now.

"I won't place any demands on you, Logan. I have to think about what's best in the long run."

He clasped her elbow. "Now, wait a minute. I'm this child's father. Any decisions we make, we make together."

She wished she could see his face in the shadows. "And what if my decisions don't coincide with yours?"

"Dammit, Meg. You've just thrown me a hand grenade. Let me absorb this. I haven't done such a great job of being a father to Travis, but I won't let you cut me out."

"You won't *let* me? *I'm* the one who's pregnant. *I'm* the one who will carry this child, decide where I want to raise it."

"Where? You can't be thinking about going back to D.C. and that life. Not with a baby."

"I don't know what I'm thinking about. But I do know that I'll never for one moment let this child think it was an accident...or a mistake. I felt like that all my life. With or without you, I'm going to love this child every minute of every hour of every day.'' Shivering, she suddenly felt cold from head to toe.

Logan slid his hand from her elbow to her fingers. ''You're cold. Let's go inside.''

Pulling away from him, she said, ''I haven't told Lily yet, and I don't intend to. At least, not right now. I don't want her to worry. She doesn't need the stress.''

''Meg, she knows you. She'll be able to tell something is wrong.''

Meg's teeth chattered, and she couldn't seem to be able to do anything about it.

''Let's go to my place. Travis won't be home for a few hours. We'll talk this through....''

Contrary to her usual opinion, talking wouldn't help this. His first reaction had been the important one. It was obvious he wasn't happy about her news. It was obvious he didn't love her. ''I think you should go home. Give us both time to sleep on it. I didn't get any sleep last night, and my thoughts keep going around in circles.'' One thought. She loved Logan. Logan didn't love her.

''Are you sure that's what you want?''

What she wanted and what she'd get were two different things. She loved Logan so much it hurt. Standing here, pretending her heart wasn't breaking, was simply too difficult. ''That's what I want.''

They walked back to the house, not touching, not talking. When Logan left, he didn't even kiss her good-night. Her past experience had taught her that love hurt. But she'd never, ever imagined it could hurt this much.

Logan drove and drove, trying not to think, but most of all, trying not to feel. What he wanted to do was return to Meg to tell her he'd handled everything all wrong. He'd known it as soon as he'd walked away.

Yet he wasn't sure how to handle it right!

Every instinct inside him had screamed, *Take her in your arms. Ask her to marry you.*

Another voice conflicted with instinct. The voice of the past reminded him of his mistakes, the tension, the heartache, of a marriage that didn't succeed because he'd forced his opinion on Shelley. It reminded him that Travis had been hurt and was still feeling the effects of a marriage that hadn't been strong enough.

And then there was Meg. A woman who was so damn strong and independent, she wouldn't let anyone make decisions for her or tell her what to do. But God help him, he wanted her and he wanted this child! Marrying Meg would give him so much joy....

He pushed his foot down on the accelerator. What kind of marriage could they have if she wanted to return to her career? He couldn't move to D.C. right now. He couldn't uproot Travis again. They were finally finding each other.

Damn it all to—

Logan let up on the gas. He wanted to marry Meg. Period. Somehow he had to convince her that was what she wanted, too—him, a family and a life in Willow Valley. He wouldn't stand by and let her waltz out of his life. Together they'd find a way through this. The right way.

Friday evening, the wash basket tilted over, and the clean laundry spilled onto the laundry-room floor. Meg stooped over and plopped it back in. She'd gone to the adoption agency this morning, hoping to keep herself distracted. But that had been a silly idea. There, couples wanting children and children needing parents surrounded her.

All day she'd been haunted by a familiar sadness she'd carried with her as a child. Then she'd think about the life inside her and experienced indescribable joy. Down...up. Up...down. What a day. And then trying to get through supper, pretending her life wasn't in chaos...

Suddenly Meg heard footfalls in the kitchen. They didn't belong to her aunt or uncle. If she could have fled, she would have. But the small room off the kitchen was a dead end, and she was trapped.

Logan stood in the doorway for a moment. But when she stooped to lift the wash basket, he moved. "Where do you want it?" He took it from her.

"Logan, it's not that heavy...."

"Where do you want it?"

When his jaw tensed like that, there was no point in arguing. "On the kitchen table. I have to fold it." She followed Logan to the kitchen.

He set the wash basket on the table, the lines around his mouth cutting deep as he said, "Let's go to the movies."

"What?"

"I want to take you out somewhere."

Sometimes she really believed men and women were from totally different planets. "I don't want to be taken out. If you're not ready to talk about the things we need to talk about..."

"I'm ready, all right." His eyes were the darkest green of a rain forest and just as impenetrable. "But I'm more worried about you. You're pale. You seem tense. I thought maybe we could relax, then go get something to eat and talk then.''

''I don't know, Logan.''

In a lightning-quick movement, he was before her clasping her shoulders. ''We were friends before we were lovers, weren't we?''

She wanted so much more than friendship and being lovers. She wanted the kind of love she'd witnessed between her aunt and uncle. Studying Logan's face, loving him, she couldn't stop hoping.

The movie theater, built in the strip shopping center with a large food store, jewelry store and a few smaller shops, didn't seat many moviegoers. Several people who knew Logan stopped him to chat, and his good intentions for the evening were fast fading away. Meg was already withdrawn. Each acquaintance who stopped him, usually asking about Travis, pushed her further into her shell. All he wanted to do was kiss her and remind her of the feelings between them.

As soon as they took their seats in the theater, the previews began. Meg sat stiff and straight beside him. He took her hand and tucked it into the crook of his arm. When she didn't pull away, he was relieved.

The movie was a comedy. He thought laughter would be a good icebreaker. But the shenanigans were slapstick, and he didn't laugh. Neither did Meg. Yep, this had been a *lousy* idea.

As the theater emptied after the movie, Meg stood beside Logan. ''I'm really not hungry.''

''Meg, you have to eat.''

''This isn't a good time of day for me, Logan. I'd rather just go back to Lily's and get a few crackers.''

He'd never even asked if she had morning sickness. "Fine. We'll go back." After they climbed in the car and headed to Lily's, he asked, "Do you have morning sickness, too?"

"No. Just afternoons and sometimes in the evening."

"Have you seen Doc?"

"Yes. So, I'm sure if that's what you're asking..."

"I didn't doubt you. Shelley knew almost right away—"

"I guess she was a few steps ahead of me."

He never should have brought up Shelley's name. Damn, he was handling this badly. As he drove down the lane to the farm, he asked, "Did Doc give you vitamins?"

"Logan, I know how to take care of myself and my baby!"

Pulling to a stop, he switched off the ignition. "This is *my* baby, too."

"I'm not about to forget." She unsnapped her seat belt.

He unsnapped his. "Then why are you pushing me away?"

"I'm not pushing you away. I'm trying to make it clear that I'm an intelligent woman. I love this baby already and would never do anything detrimental to it or me!"

In the rays of the porch light, he could see her independence but also the shimmering vulnerability. Without a thought of the consequences or all the things they needed to discuss, he slipped his hand behind her head and caught her lips before she could say anything else.

She tried to pull away for an instant, but when his tongue eased into the corner of her mouth, she surrendered. Logan pushed between her lips, too frustrated by the wall she'd erected to use finesse. He felt his control slipping from the first stroke of his tongue on hers. She returned his desire by inviting him deeper. He thrust inside with a primal rhythm, symbolizing the union he truly wanted. He wanted to possess all of her, coax her to open to him, to need a future with him as much as he needed one with her.

He splayed his fingers into her silky brown hair, imagining their bodies uniting again in sweet harmony. She hadn't buttoned her jacket. He needed more than kissing. When his hand slipped under her sweater, she moaned and pressed against his hand. He thrust his tongue against hers over and over, trying to show her how much he cared, how much he wanted this child . . . *their* child.

Her fingers clutching at his shoulders drove him on. He cupped her breast in his hand. It felt fuller. It felt . . .

He swore a blue streak in his mind. What in the name of good sense was he doing? Meg was pregnant with his child. This wouldn't give them answers. In fact—

Tearing away, he tried to get control of his breathing and his thoughts.

"What's the matter?" she asked in a soft voice.

"I'm sorry. This isn't going to get us anywhere. It's what got us into this mess."

For those few moments when they'd been entangled in each other's arms, the distance had faded away. Now it was back along with the night chill, which was getting frostier as each second ticked by. But even with

Meg's withdrawal, he didn't expect her to suddenly throw open the car door and hop out.

Before he could reach for her, she said, "I thought we did have something to talk about. But I was wrong. I absolve you of this mess, Logan MacDonald. It's *my* mess now. And probably the best way for me to handle it is to handle it alone." She slammed the car door so hard it rattled, the echo surprising Logan almost as much as her words and her exit. By the time he'd climbed out, she'd already gone into the house and closed the door. He didn't need gut instinct to tell him she wouldn't open it again to him tonight.

When Meg sagged against the back door, her first sob broke loose. All she could do was wrap her arms around herself and let the tears fall.

Suddenly the light went on, and Lily stood in front of her. "Meg, honey. What's wrong? Did you and Logan have a fight?"

"I'm pregnant, Aunt Lily. I thought I could handle this alone. I didn't want to worry you." Her tears felt hot on her cold cheeks, and she tried to brush them away, but they were falling too fast.

Her aunt wrapped her arms around her niece. "You don't have to handle anything alone. Especially not this. What did Logan say?"

"He thinks it's a mess. He doesn't love me."

"Did he say that?"

"He didn't have to. When I first told him...he didn't say anything. And then tonight... What is it about me? Mom and Dad couldn't love me. Neither could Todd. And now Logan..."

Her aunt stroked Meg's hair as she'd done when her niece was a child. "Unconditional love is a miracle.

We can't earn it, honey. It just is. You've known too few miracles in your life. But I do think Logan cares about you. Very much.''

Meg pulled away and swiped at her tears with her hand. She wouldn't let a man, not even Logan, do this to her. Apparently he had wanted to play. He'd wanted sex. As attracted as they'd been to each other, they'd given in to their desires. Well, now, she was left with more than desire. Her heart hurt, but he'd given her a gift.

Just as long ago, she'd accepted her parents' abandonment and found joy in her aunt and uncle's love, so now she'd accept the fact that Logan's passion was that and nothing else. Now she'd find joy in the child growing inside her. Her child would know the miracle of unconditional love.

''If Logan calls, I don't want to talk to him.''

''Do you think that's wise?''

''For now it's the wisest thing I can do. I have decisions to make, Aunt Lily. I have to center my energy on them and the baby. So, please, if he calls, tell him I'm busy. I have to pull myself together before I can face him again.''

And as she had as far back as Meg could remember, Lily gave her niece unconditional love. ''All right. But you *will* have to face him again—and soon. Knowing Logan, he won't let you hide very long.''

''Don't be so sure. He might want me to hide forever.''

Lily just shook her head and gave Meg another hug. This time she didn't pull away.

Chapter Thirteen

Meg stood in the front yard and admired her uncle's handiwork as he looped cedar garlands wrapped with twinkle lights across the front porch's banister. Lily sat on the swing bundled in a corduroy coat, watching her husband, making sure he did it "right." The pine cone wreath on the door Lily had made herself years ago. This year it wore a gold bow. After a hug for her aunt and a "good job" and a wink for her uncle, Meg went inside and hung her coat in the foyer closet, thinking about her day at the adoption center.

Her professional and personal interest in the job was becoming more involved. She enjoyed it—both the worthwhile feeling of accomplishment in placing children with loving families, and the people she worked with. It wouldn't be a stretch to imagine herself taking the position as liaison permanently. Yet, she didn't know if that decision would solve problems or create more. Did she want to stay in Willow Valley if Logan didn't love her? If he didn't truly want this child?

After she fixed herself a cup of tea, she sat at the kitchen table, trying to think about something other than children and Logan. When the doorbell rang, she peeked out behind the kitchen curtain. No sheriff's car. No navy sedan. During the past few days Logan had called several times. But she wasn't answering the phone.

As Meg opened the back door, she didn't find Logan, but rather his son. Travis had been dropping in twice a week for practice sessions, but she hadn't seen him since Thanksgiving, two weeks ago.

"Hi. You busy?" he asked without his customary smile.

She wondered what, if anything, Logan had told him. "No. I just got home. Come on in."

Shifting his backpack to the side, he lifted it off and set it on the table. "Did you and Dad have a fight?"

Before answering, she went to the cupboard and took out two glasses. "It's more complicated than a fight. I think you should ask your Dad."

Travis, as well as Logan, had become comfortable at Lily and Ned's house. The teenager pulled a carton of milk from the refrigerator. Seeing that it was skim, he turned up his nose and found the regular quart. "Dad's been a bear. I don't think he'd like a bunch of questions." After he opened the carton, he didn't pour. "Do you want me here? I mean, if you're mad at him and you'd rather not do this . . ."

"Travis, I told you before. You and I can be friends no matter what happens with me and your dad."

He studied her for a moment, then poured the milk. "It's about you going back to Washington, isn't it?"

"It's about a lot of things."

Travis pulled out a chair with his foot and sat at the table. "Dad and I have been getting along better. I mean, he still thinks he should run everything, but he's not so...I don't know. At least he doesn't jump down my throat when I go out now."

Meg knew how difficult it had been for Logan to give his son some space.

"You and Dad...you're not fighting because of me, are you? Another year, and I'll be gone."

Was this the reason Travis had really stopped by today? Meg sat across from him and didn't evade the probing question in his gaze. "Travis, you have nothing to do with my problems with your dad."

"For sure?"

She nodded. "For sure."

Travis visibly relaxed as he leaned back in his chair. "Are you going to the square dance Saturday night?"

The second weekend in December, Willow Valley fire company hosted a Christmas bazaar during the day and a square dance in the evening. Meg told Travis the truth. "I really haven't thought about it."

"Dad has a sheriff's meeting in Lynchburg, but he'll probably be back by evening."

"Is that a warning?" She smiled, not sure where Travis was headed.

"Sort of. He usually goes. I thought you'd want to know."

So now she knew. What she'd do about it was another matter entirely.

* * *

The booth beckoned to Meg on Saturday morning as she passed one stand after another displaying Christmas ornaments and handicrafts. This particular booth held a stack of homemade baby bibs, quilts and sweaters with bootees and caps. Meg picked up a tiny white crocheted sweater that was as soft as Leo's kitten fur.

"Are you going to buy it?"

Meg turned and found her uncle at her elbow. "It's a little soon."

"It's not too soon to plan and dream. I guess you know Lily's as excited about this baby as you are."

Her aunt *was* excited. She loved to nurture. "Aunt Lily and you should have had ten kids."

Ned shrugged. "It wasn't to be. When we were trying to have a family, there were no fertility drugs or in-vitro-fertilization procedures. We probably should have adopted. But we always struggled with the farm. And then again, we had you."

"And I had you."

He nodded to the baby sweater in her hand. "Now you're going to have a child of your own. That makes us proud."

"Even though I'm a single woman?"

"From what Lily tells me, you're not giving Logan much of a chance to make it otherwise." He frowned and gave her a look she'd seen before, a look that said she might be acting foolish.

"Uncle Ned..."

"Are you going to the square dance tonight?"

She knew as well as anyone else she couldn't avoid Logan forever. Tonight, in the midst of a crowd of people, would probably be the best place to see him again. They wouldn't have to "talk" unless they both made a concerted effort.

Whenever she thought about Logan, she ached for what might have been. "Yes, I'm going tonight. You and Aunt Lily would probably carry me if I said I wasn't."

Her uncle chuckled and gestured to the sweater. "So, are you going to buy that?"

Meg smiled. It *was* time to dream and plan, at least about her baby. "Yes, I am. And I might buy a few bibs, too. I hear babies go through quite a few."

Logan's tie had gotten tighter as the day-long meeting had droned on. Finally at home, he tugged it loose and tossed it over his bedroom chair. His shirt followed.

Travis stopped in the doorway. "I'm leaving."

"For the square dance?"

"We'll get there eventually. A couple of stops first."

Logan opened his mouth, then closed it again.

Travis grinned. "Very good, Dad. You didn't ask if we were stopping for booze. I gotta split. If I pretend I don't know you at the fire hall..."

"I know. I shouldn't take it personally."

Travis tapped his fingers on the doorframe. "You're learning, Dad. See ya."

Logan unbuckled his belt and unzipped his trousers. Yeah, he was learning, all right. Very slowly. The problem was that learning took patience, and he was about out of patience where Meg was concerned. He knew he should tell Travis that Meg was pregnant. But he was supposed to be a role model for his son. Until he and Meg reached some kind of agreement . . .

Agreement. Yeah. When she wouldn't talk to him. Well, that was going to end tonight. And if she didn't put in an appearance at the dance, he'd drive to the farm and insist she talk to him. He wouldn't leave until she did. He didn't blame her for being angry. But she'd misinterpreted what he'd meant. Granted, *mess* hadn't been the best term to use, and he'd kicked himself for the past two weeks for using it.

He understood her anger at his insensitivity, but he didn't understand her withdrawal. They'd always been able to talk. She'd always been open, coaxing *him* to lay everything out on the table. Without Meg, he might have lost his son. Maybe he hadn't told her often enough how grateful he was. How glad he was she'd come into his life. Out of all the things he should have told her, the one very important one was that he was glad she was carrying his baby. Maybe once she knew that, marriage wouldn't be such a big jump. After all, maybe he needed to court her.

What did a man wear to court a woman?

He'd think about it in the shower.

In a few hours, the social hall of the fire company had been transformed from a Christmas bazaar into a festive, barnlike atmosphere with bales of hay, cedar garlands, red ribbons, and holly centerpieces abounding. Meg sat beside Lily and Ned at one of the long tables. Friends of her aunt and uncle sat at the table with them. The band tuned up, and soon the caller stood at the microphone directing the dancers.

Meg kept her eyes on the door. Logan hadn't yet appeared. But suddenly someone stood behind her chair with a hand on her shoulder. She turned and found Michael Holden, his jeans and red plaid shirt giving him a different persona than his principal's white shirt and tie.

The chair beside her was empty. He nodded to it. "Do you mind?"

"No. Have a seat. How are you?"

"Good. Is Logan here?"

She shrugged as nonchalantly as she could manage. "Not that I know of."

He looked at her curiously. "Is something wrong?"

His concern made her give him an honest answer. "Nothing I want to talk about."

Smiling, he said, "All right. Then I'll assume you came tonight to have fun. Are you having it yet?"

Michael really was a nice man, and she had to smile back. "Not quite yet."

He laughed. "Would you like something to eat? They have quite a spread over there. Hot dogs to popcorn."

"Just some soda. Something without caffeine."

After Michael brought them two glasses of soda, he asked, "Would you like to join a square?"

She'd asked Doc about exercise. He'd told her what she'd suspected—keeping fit was the best way to keep problems during pregnancy to a minimum. "Yes, I would."

As Meg do-si-doed with Michael, she remembered the fun she'd had as a teenager when she'd gone to square dances. It was the challenge of hearing the calls and keeping her feet moving in the right direction. It was the mixture of male and female, brushing elbows, laughing and misstepping that put everyone in a congenial mood. But when the caller directed her to promenade with her partner and Michael took her hand, she longed for Logan beside her. She longed to be sharing the moments of fun with him.

On a deeper level, she realized she wanted him beside her through her pregnancy and during the birth of their child. Her heart ached because she knew she wanted something from him he couldn't give. Because of Shelley. Because of Travis. He'd probably never expected to be a father again. With the heartache and turmoil he'd gone through the past few years with Travis, contemplating the responsibilities of fatherhood again was probably just too painful. Yet she knew Logan was the type of man whose sense of responsibility was as vital to him as his sense of duty. Essentially that's why she'd been hiding from him. She was afraid his sense of responsibility or duty would trap him again in a life he didn't want.

For that reason, she'd kept the idea of going back to D.C. as an option. On the other hand, if she took the liaison position with Victoria's adoption agency, Logan would have access to his child if he wanted it. As much as she'd thought about what was best for her and the baby, she'd thought about what was best for Logan, too. Because she loved him.

But loving him only added confusion to questions that seemed to have no answers.

When the song was over, Michael nudged her elbow. "You stopped smiling. For a while there, I thought you might be having fun."

"For a while, I was. Do you think scientists have ever done a study on how detrimental thinking can be to a person's health?"

He took her hand and positioned her across from him in another square. "The secret is to keep too busy

to think. Now, what do you say we try this again until
you get it right?''

Michael's patient amusement was contagious. ''All
right. Let's give it one more try.''

He squeezed her shoulder. ''That a girl.''

Before the music started again, Cal walked by the
square, saw Meg and Michael facing each other and
frowned. Stepping closer to Michael, but not so far
away that Meg couldn't hear, he warned in a low voice,
''She's the sheriff's lady, Holden. You better not get
any poaching ideas if you know what's good for you.''

Meg stood stunned.

Michael responded to the deputy sheriff calmly.
''Then I guess the sheriff should be a little more at-
tentive to his lady if he expects other men *not* to get
any ideas.''

Cal scowled, but when Michael wasn't intimidated,
the deputy arched his brows at Meg and walked away.

Meg finally found her voice. ''I don't believe he said
that.''

''One thing Cal is is loyal.''

''Loyalty is one thing. That kind of...of...outdated
chauvinism is another.''

''We're in Willow Valley, Meg.''

The music started; the caller called the dance. And
Meg made up her mind she was definitely going to
have fun.

The fun stopped cold when she felt Logan's gaze on
her. How could she tell he'd arrived when the room
was full of people? The question was moot. She just
could. He stood beside a stack of bales of hay, his
arms crossed over his chest. His black jeans, gray,
western-cut shirt and black boots made him look tall,
dangerous and as sexy as she could ever remember him

looking. Her hormones were just in a whirl from her pregnancy. That had to explain why, out of all the men in the room, she only felt an overwhelming attraction toward Logan. She ignored it. She was having fun.

Sure, it was lots of fun to see Cal stop beside his boss and mumble something to him. Logan frowned, looked at Michael, then back at her. Not hard to imagine what *that* was about.

It was lots of fun to wonder if she'd split a seam. She'd worn the puffed-sleeved turquoise blouse and matching full skirt, knowing it would be comfortable if she felt like dancing. Logan was looking at her so hard... what was the phrase he'd used at the fund-raiser? *Undressing her with his eyes.*

And it was the most fun to imagine what would happen when the dance was over. Would he come to her? Should she go to him? It was a shame she knew how to square dance so well. Obviously she wasn't busy enough to stop thinking.

When the dance ended, she didn't have to imagine what would happen next. Logan pushed himself away from the bales of hay and headed right toward her, a scowl drawing his brows together.

He stopped a few inches from her. "Do you think you should be doing this?"

As if Michael sensed something in Logan that could be intimidating, he protectively laid a hand on Meg's shoulder. "Why shouldn't she?"

Logan's gaze pointedly stayed on Michael Holden's hand. "Because she's pregnant, and this kind of activity could be harmful to our baby." There was the slightest emphasis on the word "our."

Meg was mortified, and Michael's look of astonishment didn't help. "Logan! I can't believe you'd

embarrass me like this. If you think this macho behavior is going to help anything, you're mistaken."

Michael dropped his hand from her shoulder.

Logan curved his arm around her and nudged her
toward the closest exit. "I want to talk to you."

She dug in her heels and wouldn't move. "Maybe I
don't want to talk to *you*."

"Do I have to pick you up and carry you?"

One look at his face told her that's exactly what he'd
do. "All right."

He guided her toward the back exit, out onto a
landing. She shivered and rubbed her arms.

"We should have gotten your coat."

"I'm fine."

"You're *always* fine. That's the problem!"

"And just what is that supposed to mean?"

He looked as if he wanted to shake her...or kiss her.
She wasn't sure which. "It means you don't always
have to handle everything yourself. It means that this
is *our* child you're carrying. It means I want you to
marry me."

It was a demand, not a request or a proposal. Hurt,
she said the first thought that came to mind. "The
same way you wanted Shelley to marry you?"

He exploded. "No!" With a slash of his hand
through the air, he said angrily, "You're not Shelley."

"No, but I bet the reasons you want me to marry
you are the same ones that made you ask Shelley."

"No."

"Logan, the situation is the same."

He stuffed his hands in his pockets. "I want to give
our baby a family. I know I've made mistakes with
Travis, but I won't repeat them with this child."

Logan's intentions were good, but his motivation lacked what she needed most—his love. "You can be a good father without marrying me. I won't keep the baby from you. I couldn't—"

Logan's pager beeped, then beeped again. The string of epithets he uttered should have scandalized her. But they didn't. He was angry and frustrated. She felt like yelling a few choice swear words herself. Maybe then she wouldn't feel like fleeing to her room at Lily and Ned's and having a good cry.

"I have to call in. Go inside where it's warm. I'll find you."

"Logan, do you know how to do anything but give orders?" she flared.

He clasped her chin with his thumb and index finger. "Yes. I know how to kiss you and touch you until you want me as much as I want you."

His honesty excited her and created pictures of the two of them together she'd never forget. But right now that picture hurt so much.... "There's more to life than sex," she said in a low voice.

Blowing out a breath, Logan opened the door and waited for her to go inside.

A few minutes later, he found her sitting with Lily and Ned. "There's been another break-in at the high school. This one's messier. Broken glass everywhere. I've got to go. If I'm tied up too late tonight, I *will* see you tomorrow. And I won't accept excuses from Lily."

With that promise, he headed for the exit.

Lily leaned her shoulder against Meg's. "I think Logan's jealous. You should have seen his face when you were dancing with Michael."

Frustrated and angry herself, she crossed one leg over the other and swung it. "He told Michael I'm pregnant."

A hint of a smile played on her aunt's lips. "He's laying claim."

"He embarrassed me!"

"You won't be more embarrassed when you start showing and everyone knows?"

Small-town thinking at its finest. She expected her aunt to be more broad-minded. "That is *no* reason to get married!"

"Married? Did I mention marriage?" Lily asked innocently.

"No, but Logan did and . . ." Her aunt's expression was expectant. "Never mind. I'm going to get another glass of soda."

Lily patted Meg's hand. "When you want to talk, honey, I'll be here."

"I appreciate it, Aunt Lily. Everything just hurts too much right now."

At the snack stand, Meg saw Travis. But he didn't see her. He was shifting from one foot to the other, watching the front door.

"Travis, are you looking for your dad? He had to leave because of a break-in at the high school."

Travis avoided her gaze. "Yeah, I know. I'm waiting for some friends."

Intuition she'd relied on over the years made her ask, "Kyle?"

"Uh, yeah." Travis was fidgety. He pulled down his T-shirt and stuffed one hand in his pocket.

"What's happening?" she asked.

"Nothing," he mumbled.

"Have you been drinking?"

"No!" He glanced at the door again. "If I tell you anything, you'll tell Dad."

"Maybe *you* should tell him."

"No way. I don't rat on friends."

She grabbed his arm. "Travis..."

Pulling away, he shook his head. "I said too much already. Forget it, Meg. Please?"

She didn't want to lose his trust. Her friendship with Logan's son had become important to her. "Only if you promise to call me if you need help with something."

"I don't need help."

"Promise me, Travis."

He didn't deny it again, but nodded. "All right. But now I gotta go."

His reassurance didn't make her feel any better, and she suddenly realized worry would be a constant part of a mother's life.

Meg had been holding her breath since she'd awakened Sunday morning, expecting to hear Logan's car crunch down the lane. But the crunch she heard didn't belong to Logan. She took a look out the back door and called to her aunt and uncle, who were reading the Sunday paper in the living room.

"Aunt Lily. Uncle Ned. Come here. It's Carmen and Manuel." Meg ran out to the truck.

Manuel hopped out first and went around to the other side of the truck to help his wife. Meg reached the truck just as Carmen handed Tomás to her husband.

Seeing Meg, Manuel grinned. "We promised we'd stop on our way to Florida."

Meg gave Carmen a hug, then turned to the baby who'd brought her and Logan together. "Yes, you did. I can't believe how much he's grown. Can I hold him?"

Without hesitation, Carmen said, "*Sí. Tú le eres especial.*"

"He's very special to me, too," Meg responded, her eyes filling up. Babies were hope and joy and laughter. So why did she feel as if her heart were tearing in two?

An hour later, she'd finally handed Tomás back to his mother. While Ned, Lily, Carmen and Manuel visited in the living room, Meg offered to make tea. She was taking low-fat muffins out of the pastry holder when a knock came at the back door. Her stomach tightened.

When she opened the door, Travis stood there. And he didn't look good. She pulled him inside. "What's wrong?"

"It's Kyle. I think he's gonna do something stupid."

"How do you know?"

"Last night, before the square dance, he'd been drinking. He said he had things to do and couldn't go with the rest of us. When I heard about the break-in, I was afraid he'd done it. But I didn't know. I was hoping he'd show up at the dance. But he didn't. Then he called me this morning and said he might not see me again for a while. He wouldn't answer my questions about where he was last night. Just said he was stopping at Gibson's, then taking off. I might be all wrong, but I think he needs money. Everybody knows old man Gibson keeps Saturday and Sunday's deposits till Monday morning."

"Why didn't you go to your dad?"

"Because I don't know where he is. He got in late last night and left a note for me this morning saying he had to talk to me but he was following up on a lead first. I didn't want to alert the whole sheriff's department. Maybe Kyle's just going to buy stuff, and then I'd look like an idiot...."

"Wait right here. I'll tell Aunt Lily I'm going out for a bit. We'll go warn Mr. Gibson, then find your father."

Chapter Fourteen

When Meg opened the door to Gibson's Grocery and walked inside, she felt as if she'd traveled back in time. All those weeks ago. Costa Rica... She saw Olan Gibson's face and remembered the panic, the terror, the nightmares. Before she could prevent Travis from coming in behind her, a voice came from her right.

"Don't move, or someone will get hurt."

She automatically went still.

"Kyle, what the hell...?" Travis turned toward the voice.

When Travis started for Kyle, Meg grabbed his hand and said, "Stop, Travis."

The teenager wore a ski mask and raised the gun in his hand. "Very good, Miss Dawson."

Travis moved toward his friend again. "You don't know what you're doing!"

Kyle raised the gun and shot at a row of canned goods at Travis's left.

Meg wanted to scream, but instead she caught Travis's elbow and held him in place with every ounce of strength in her body.

The sound of the shot had startled Travis, and he finally froze.

She laid her hand protectively over her stomach. Somehow she had to protect her baby and Travis. Somehow she had to get them out of this. What she'd feared most had happened, and she hadn't even gone back to work. One of life's ironies. She needed a clear head. She had to take one step at a time.

"What do you want, Kyle?" she asked calmly, although every nerve in her body trembled.

He tore the ski mask from his head. "I wanted this to be nice and easy. I just wanted Gibson's money, that's all."

The teenager looked as if he'd been drinking. That could slow his reflexes, but also make him more volatile.

"So, take it and go," she suggested reasonably.

He smirked. "Yeah, right. With all of you knowing who I am. I wouldn't get a block."

"You won't get a block anyway, not when my dad finds out what's going on." Anger emanated from Travis.

"Travis, cool down," Meg advised.

"While someone who's supposed to be my friend is holding a gun on me?" he snapped.

"She's right, MacDonald. You'd better pipe down till I figure out what to do." He waved the gun at Olan. "Over here with them, old man. And don't do anything you're going to regret."

* * *

Logan was asking Kyle's mother questions and listening to her problems when he got the call. His blood turned to ice as Cal gave him the specifics as he knew them. Meg, Travis and Olan Gibson were locked in the store with Kyle. Kyle had already fired a shot, and Logan didn't want to think about what that could mean.

He took off at a run and jumped into the sheriff's cruiser. Then he took his gun and holster from the locked glove compartment and strapped it on. Chances were he was going to need it. Calling the rescue-squad dispatcher, he gave instructions for them to drive to the grocery store without sirens. In case someone had been hurt, he wanted them there. But he didn't want to shake up Kyle or give him any reason to shoot again.

As Logan switched on his flashing lights and sped to Main Street, he thought over his conversation with Kyle's mother. A father who'd walked out. A mother trying to make ends meet for herself and three kids on a secretary's salary. Kyle being frustrated by not having the things he saw other teenagers had.

Last night, as Logan had interviewed witnesses concerning the second high-school break-in, he'd discovered someone had recognized Kyle running from the school. But Kyle had never returned home last night. Logan tried to will his heart to slow, tried to wipe the pictures from his mind of Travis or Meg wounded...or worse.

Life could turn on a dime. Just last night, he'd asked Meg to marry him. Just last night, he'd hoped...

He still had hope. He wouldn't lose her or either of his children.

A crowd had gathered outside the grocery store. Logan parked along the side of the building, rather than in the front. He could do this one of three ways. He could try to make contact with Kyle by phone and talk him into some kind of trade. He could surround the store in a SWAT-team-like maneuver and hope for a clear shot. He could use the back entrance of the store, go in and try to disarm Kyle himself.

On-site, he instructed five of his deputies to surround the front of the store but to wait for further orders. Then he told Cal he intended to go in the rear entrance and asked him to cover him and act as a backup. Cal followed Logan inside.

Guns drawn, Logan and Cal eased through the storeroom, careful not to make a sound. Logan stopped behind the swinging door and listened.

"So tell me why you need the money, Kyle."

That was Meg's sweet voice, calm without a quaver. Surely she was okay if she sounded like that.

"I need to get out of here. To go to Richmond like Travis. There was practically nothing in that school last night. Change. Five bucks in petty cash at the secretary's desk. Cripes, it wasn't worth the commotion of getting in."

"I told you before, Kyle, Richmond's no dream place. Even if you get a few hundred dollars, it won't go far," Travis warned.

"You managed four months on a little bit of nothing. I'll get a job," Kyle argued.

"You don't have a high-school diploma," Meg argued softly. "What kind of job are you going to get?"

"Shut up," Kyle yelled.

The silence almost killed Logan. He edged closer to the window in the door and peered through.

The teenager shook the gun at Meg. "I saw the sheriff kissing you. He'll pay to get you out of here. Hell, if he could afford a private investigator for Travis here..."

Logan watched Kyle swing the barrel of the gun near Meg's chin. All he wanted to do was lunge out of that storeroom and take the kid down. But he knew better. At least, his head did. His heart was screaming for him to act. If anything happened to Travis or Meg... Lord, how he loved them both.

Love... love... love.

The word echoed, making his head spin and his heart pound even harder. Of course he loved her. That's why he wanted to marry her. Couldn't she see that? Couldn't she see...

He fought against the swell of feelings.

Right now he needed to alert her to his presence.

When he carefully checked the window again, Kyle's back was to him. Logan stood at the small window, praying Meg would look beyond Kyle and see him. But all her attention was riveted on the teenager.

He couldn't make a sound. That would alert Kyle. But if he could make some small motion... He tested the swinging door. No sound. He pushed it a little farther. Still no sound. Now, if she would just look.

Suddenly Meg lifted her chin a fraction of an inch. Her gaze went from the doorframe to Logan's face at the window. Then she dropped her gaze again to Kyle's gun.

"Kyle, if you want money, then you're going to have to do something about it. Why don't we go over to the phone and call the sheriff's office? If I could talk to Logan and tell him we're all fine..."

She was a sweetheart, all right, giving him the information he needed to hear most.

"Why are you in such an all-fired hurry to help me?" Kyle exploded.

"Because I'm afraid. And Travis and Mr. Gibson probably are, too. That gun's dangerous, Kyle."

"Yeah, and I know how to use it."

"I can tell Logan that. I can tell him..." She stopped for a moment. "I can tell him you don't want to hurt us, that you just want to get out."

Kyle looked confused. "I need a car."

"I can tell him that, too. In fact, you can tell him. But we have to go over there to the phone."

Logan caught on to what she was doing. She was putting their lives in his hands. To get to the phone, she and Kyle would have to pass the door. He'd have a split second to take Kyle down before he could hurt anyone. Meg trusted him that much. Yet she didn't want to marry him.

"C'mon, Kyle. Let's get this over with. You don't want to hurt us. I know you don't," Meg urged. Her soft voice, her wide brown eyes, her caring attitude, seemed to work on the teenager.

"You're not trying to trick me," he said as if he was trying to convince himself.

"No tricks. I don't know any tricks, Kyle. But I do want to ask a favor. Why don't you let Travis and Mr. Gibson leave? You don't need them. You have me."

"You *are* trying to trick me."

"I'm staying with you," Travis announced with the same protectiveness Logan felt.

Meg was trying to get Gibson and Travis out of harm's way. But it wasn't working. Logan's quick glance at Olan Gibson told him the older man was shell-shocked. He was probably afraid he'd do or say something that would make matters worse.

"All of you are staying," Kyle decided, waving the gun. "Gibson, Travis, you move and I shoot. You got it?" he demanded.

Olan nodded, but Travis said between clenched teeth, "So help me, Kyle, if I ever get my hands on you…"

"Yeah, well, you're not going to, Travis. C'mon, Miss Dawson. I want five thousand dollars and a car. In an hour. A sheriff should have enough clout for that."

"You could just put down the gun, Kyle," she suggested. "It would go a lot easier for you."

"Quit yakking. Let's make the call."

Logan readied himself. All of his years in law enforcement, the rigors of keeping fit, the afternoons at the shooting range, his love for Meg, their unborn child and Travis, boiled down to this one moment. He wouldn't have another. She'd done all she could as the intelligent, gutsy woman she was. Now he had to make this maneuver work or regret it the rest of his life.

Meg passed the door first, as Logan knew she would. He caught a glimpse of her hair through the window. And then he listened and watched for a shadow…

All at once, Kyle stepped in front of the door. Logan slammed it open into the teenager with the force of a tornado. A shot hit the wall.

"Everyone on the floor," Logan yelled.

Then Logan pinned Kyle's arms behind his back, and Cal was there, cuffing the teenager. Olan Gibson must have opened the front door, because the other deputies rushed in.

Meg was sitting on Olan's stool behind the counter, her face pale, her hands gripping the counter.

As the deputies escorted Kyle out, Logan hurried to her. "Are you all right?"

She looked up. "I'm fine. I..."

"Dad!"

Logan threw his arms around his son. "Are *you* all right?"

He held on tight, thinking about how close he'd come to almost losing the two people he cared about the most in this world. Holding on was more important than breathing or talking or anything else.

Finally Travis pulled away. "That was so cool, Dad. Did Meg know you were there? How did she..."

When Logan looked over at Meg... she was gone! "Where did she go?"

"I don't know. She was here."

They both rushed outside and caught a glimpse of her in the front seat of someone's car as it drove away. Logan's heart pounded as it had when he'd stood behind the door. "She probably wanted to get home so Lily and Ned would know she's all right."

"What's going on with you two, Dad?"

Logan took a deep breath, feeling as if he needed a few hundred more to slow his adrenaline. "Meg's pregnant."

"Wow!"

"Yeah, wow," Logan repeated wryly.

"Ya know, Dad, maybe you and I should have a discussion about the birds, the bees and condoms."

Logan could feel his cheeks flush. "Things got out of hand, we got caught up in the moment."

Travis grinned. "I think I've heard that stuff from a few guys I know."

"Look, I know I'm a lousy role model where this is concerned."

Travis's grin faded. "What's going to happen? I mean, you said you didn't really love Mom when you asked her to marry you."

"I know. And at first I compared this situation to that one. But they're very different. I was committed to your mother, Travis, and I cared about her deeply. But with Meg . . . I *do* love her. How would you feel if we got married?"

"I like Meg. I think . . . we're friends. It would even be kinda neat."

Logan slung his arm around his son's shoulders. "Travis, I need to know exactly what happened last night and this morning, whatever you know about Kyle."

Travis looked up at his father. "You don't think I was in cahoots with Kyle, do you? Because I wasn't."

Logan knew his answer would shape their relationship for years to come. He looked into his son's eyes, saw the truth there and said, "If you say you weren't, I believe you. I just need you to fill in missing pieces if you can."

"You really believe me?"

"Yes."

Travis relaxed. "I'll tell you whatever I can."

As they walked to the car, Travis asked, "Dad, can you do anything for Kyle? He just wanted to get out of Willow Valley. I mean, I know what he did today was bad, but *he's* not. Do you know what I mean?"

Logan knew exactly what his son meant. If someone could have helped Kyle before he'd gotten this desperate... "I can't make any promises. But I'll try to get him some help. Okay?"

"Okay."

When Logan removed his arm from Travis's shoulders, his son said, "You know, Dad, that's the first time you've hugged me since I was twelve."

Logan's chest tightened. "Then it was long overdue. And I'm warning you right now, it won't be long till the next one."

Travis grimaced, but Logan watched the grimace change into a small smile. His son was finally home.

Meg knew she had run away again, telling herself she had to get home so her aunt and uncle would realize she was safe and unharmed. And she did. But she'd also needed time to get her thoughts together before she talked to Logan.

She sat on the edge of the guest-room bed, watching Tomás sleep in his cradle, the cradle she'd once slept in. Family, friends and tradition meant so much. And the love that surrounded all of it...

So much had become clear to her the moment her gaze had met Logan's at Gibson's Grocery. She'd risk her life for Travis and the baby she carried; she'd risk her life for Logan. No love could burn deeper than that.

Logan had done his job this afternoon. Had it been more than his job? Had love shown them how to communicate, to make the split-second timing work? She wouldn't know until she asked. She wouldn't know until she found the courage to tell Logan she loved him and discovered how he felt in return.

And if he didn't love her?

Her heart would break. But she'd also hold on to the hope that staying in Willow Valley, parenting their child together, would eventually give him the freedom to love. She'd stay here and love him. But she wouldn't marry him unless he could offer her more than a fulfillment of responsibility.

Long ago she'd learned facing life's challenges required courage. She had the courage to stay in Willow Valley and stop running from whatever Logan did feel for her. Maybe someday it would turn into love.

The crunch of tires on gravel urged her to switch her gaze from Tomás to the window. Logan.

Now all she had to do was find the courage to tell him she loved him.

Still wearing his uniform, Logan sat on the swing on Lily's front porch absently gazing at the Christmas decorations, waiting for Meg. Lily had said Meg was upstairs tucking Tomás in for his nap. Logan wanted to see the couple and their baby, but first he had to talk to the woman he loved and give her a symbol of that love, along with the words he should have said before now.

His thoughts had been in turmoil since Meg had told him she was pregnant. He'd realized why today in the midst of the chaos. He loved her. The problem was— he hadn't offered her love. He'd offered her passion, caring, marriage. But Meg had needed more. She'd needed his love.

Suddenly this afternoon, with her life on the line, he'd figured out why she'd withdrawn from him when once she'd been so open. Essentially Meg's parents had abandoned her. Although she was a warm, compassionate woman, she didn't trust easily. Somehow, between the birth of Manuel and Carmen's baby and Logan's problems with Travis, she'd started to trust him. And hopefully love him. She'd never said it, and now he knew why. Her saying it would be the ultimate risk, a plea for her love to be returned.

Not only had her parents abandoned her, but so had a man she'd loved. Once again work, rather than emotions, had been important. When Logan had met Meg, both their guards had slipped. Desire and feelings had become inseparable. When she'd told him she was pregnant, he'd thought he was doing the best thing by not pushing her, by not *trapping* her. Yet his silence and distance had given her another message that she'd again read as abandonment, and if not that, his lack of love.

He could see it all so clearly now.

The most important question was, had he blown his chances with the lady he loved?

He'd soon know. The pine cone wreath rattled as the door opened. He stopped pushing the swing with his foot and drank in the sight of Meg in her colorful wool jacket and stirrup pants.

When she stepped down on the porch, he stood. "You ran away."

She blushed. "I realized so much in the midst of everything that happened. I needed time to think about it."

Where before he'd made a mistake by not telling her his feelings, right now he sensed she needed to talk about hers. "What did you think about?"

She searched his face as if she was looking for something special. "I'm no longer afraid to go back to work. I faced my worst fear today and did it successfully. I have a feeling the nightmares will stop, too.''

His heart did a nosedive and the ring he'd bought a half hour ago became a weight in his pocket. "I see. Does that mean you'll be moving back to D.C.?''

She looked hesitant but took a step closer to him. "No. It means I won't be moving back. When our lives were in danger today, I also realized nothing is more important to me than this baby... and you and Travis.''

Hope flared again, and he stepped so close to her they were almost touching. "You trusted me with your life today, but I think you're still afraid to trust me with your heart. That's my fault, and I'm sorry. I just hope it's not too late.''

"Too late for what?'' she murmured, her brown eyes wide and soft and maybe just a bit hopeful.

"For me to tell you how much I love you. Yes, I want to marry you for the sake of our child, but also because we're good together in bed and out. We can talk and kiss and argue. I think that's because we love each other so completely. Travis was willing to stay in the situation and risk his life for you. You were willing to risk your life for Travis. And I wouldn't have had a life if anything happened to either of you. I'm asking you to marry me so I can give you the love you deserve—a love that accepts who you are and what you need, a love that will last forever.''

Tears fell down her cheeks. "Lily calls that kind of love a miracle.''

He couldn't keep from wrapping his arms around Meg and pulling her into his body. Stroking her hair, he asked, "What do you think?''

Meg lifted her head and tenderly traced his jaw. "I think I'm trying to get up the courage to stop running and hiding from you." Her lower lip quivered as she said, "I love you, Logan. More than I thought it possible to love anyone. Even after this afternoon, a little voice in my head kept saying, 'He only did his job.' But my heart knew better. It has all along. That's why making love with you is a miracle in itself."

He'd never known a woman more loving or honest or courageous than Margaret Elizabeth Dawson. Taking the ring from his pocket, he clasped her hand and slipped the solitaire diamond on her finger.

She looked at the ring with a radiant smile. "It's beautiful."

As her gaze returned to his with so much love it overwhelmed him, there was only one more way he knew how to tell her how much he loved her. He kissed her forehead, her eyes, her cheeks. When she lifted her lips to his, he took her tenderly until their love exploded into passion they couldn't deny. Sweeping her off her feet, he carried her to the swing, where he held her in his lap. Their eyes sent loving messages, their tongues explored, their hands crept to warm places until finally Logan raised his head.

Surrounding her with his arms, loving her tucked into his body, he said, "You haven't answered my question. Will you marry me?"

She held his face between her hands, running her fingers along his jaw. "Yes, I'll marry you."

Suddenly she looked worried.

"Sweetheart, what's wrong?"

"Travis. How do you think he'll feel?"

Logan passed his hand up and down her arm, almost afraid to believe his heart's desire was within his grasp. "He approves. And he understands that I love you. He understands we're not getting married just for the sake of the baby."

"You told him?"

He lifted her chin and smoothed the pad of his thumb over the delicate point. "I'm ready to tell the world."

With the sweetest smile he'd ever seen, she set her lips on his, traced their outline with her tongue, then pulled away. "There's a town-council meeting tomorrow night. We can do it then," she teased.

"I'd rather do 'it' right now."

Her expression was smug and thoroughly seductive at the same time. "Why, Sheriff MacDonald! We're on the front porch of my aunt and uncle's house."

He lowered his lips to her ear and said in a low voice, "I'd remedy that and carry you to the barn if you didn't have company."

Bracing her hands on his chest, she promised, "You can carry me to the barn later, after we visit with our company."

"Do you think Lily and Ned will let us borrow their barn after we're married?"

"I'm sure of it."

He looked into her eyes, so full of everything he wanted to see and more. "I love you, Meg. Will you marry me soon? Before the holidays so we can share Christmas with everyone we love as husband and wife?" He couldn't keep the husky note of possession from his voice.

"Nothing would make me happier than sharing Christmas with you as your wife."

Logan found her lips again . . . giving, taking and sharing their love—their miracle.

Epilogue

Meg clapped her hands and tried to keep her tears in check as Travis received his college diploma. "I'm going to miss him," she murmured to Logan.

"Sweetheart, he's been gone for four years," her husband responded reasonably.

Four-and-a-half-year-old Suzanne, sitting on her mother's lap, clapped her hands, too. "He's goin' *far* away."

Logan slipped his arm around his wife's shoulders. "He's wanted to go back to Spain since he spent half of his senior year there in high school. Only now he'll have a job. Remember when *you* used to enjoy traveling?"

Travis had earned a degree in international finance, as well as majoring in Spanish. The two had gotten him an entry-level position with an American corporation based in Spain.

Chun Won slipped from the folding chair and tried to wave at his brother as he came down from the platform set up in the center of the football field. Even from the considerable distance, Meg saw Travis give them a thumbs-up sign.

She smoothed her hand over Chun Won's coal black hair. After Suzanne was born, Meg had worked part time at Victoria's agency, taking her daughter along with her. Then one day, two years ago, Chun Won's file had come across her desk. Meg had read that he'd been abandoned at birth and left at a Korean orphanage. She and Logan adopted him. He'd needed tons of love and affection, something she and Logan had plenty to give. From the day he'd arrived in the United States, she'd decided to stay home full time, although she still helped Victoria when she got into a bind.

Remembering her husband's question about traveling, she teased, "You and the children are enough of an adventure." She felt the familiar kick of the newest member of their family residing in her womb.

"When we get home, I have a surprise for you." Logan's smile was slightly off center and mysterious.

"What?"

"If I tell you, it won't be a surprise."

She laid her hand on his muscled thigh and gave it a squeeze. "Tell me."

Green passion, deep and exciting, intensified in Logan's eyes. It was still like that between them. A smile, a touch, and they wanted each other as much as they had the first time they'd made love, whether they were in their own bed or in her aunt and uncle's barn.

He chuckled. "Are you going to use coercion?"

"If I have to," she assured him with a coy smile that she knew would raise the stakes a notch or two.

Leaning toward her, he gave her a sound kiss that made the beautiful May day in Connecticut even more memorable.

When Logan pulled away, she asked, "Was that supposed to distract me?"

"No. That was supposed to tell you how much I love you."

He never forgot to tell her or show her...often. The past five years had taught her she could depend on love and believe in its power to solve any problem and forge a bond so strong Logan's heart and hers communicated without words.

Stroking her cheek, he smiled. "The plans are finished for the new house. We can pick them up from the contractor when we get home."

That was a surprise. She hadn't expected them for another two weeks. "Our dream house."

"And a house to dream in."

Logan understood her dreams as well as he understood her. Best of all, he shared them.

She remembered back to a day when she was twelve, standing on her aunt's porch. Then, she'd decided she belonged in Willow Valley. Now she called Willow Valley home, but she knew she belonged with Logan.

Until the end of time.

Suzanne laid her dark head on Meg's shoulder. Chun Won stationed himself between her and Logan, leaning against his father's knee. The graduation ceremony complete, Travis walked toward them, his robe flapping in the breeze.

Love blessed her daily with its miracles.

Logan took her hand and held it tightly in his. Their love was the greatest miracle of all.

* * * * *

COMING NEXT MONTH

#1075 A LAWMAN FOR KELLY—Myrna Temte
That Special Woman!
U.S. marshal meets gal from the wrong side of the law. Result?
Arresting display of sparks until that special woman Kelly Jaynes
finally gets her man—handsome lawman Steve Anderson!

#1076 MISTAKEN BRIDE—Brittany Young
Kate Fairfax had always had a troubled relationship with her identical
twin. So when her sister asked her to be at her wedding, Kate was
happy to attend. But she *never* expected to be so attracted to the
groom...or that the upcoming wedding would be her own!

#1077 LIVE-IN MOM—Laurie Paige
Love was in the air the moment Carly Lightfoot and Ty Macklin set
eyes on each other. Ty had a ranch and a son to look out for, and
didn't have time for romance—that is, until Ty's son decided Carly
would make a perfect mom and schemed to get her together with his
dad....

#1078 THE LONE RANGER—Sharon De Vita
Silver Creek County
Texas Ranger Cody Kincaid had come to Silver Creek to get the job
done—protect widowed Savannah Duncan and her son from someone
trying to scare her off her land. But he didn't bargain on getting so
attached to the sexy single mom and her mischievous child. Whether
Cody knew it or not, this lone ranger needed a family....

#1079 MR. FIX-IT—Jo Ann Algermissen
Finding themselves working side by side was an unexpected bonus
for Brandon Corral and Molly Winsome. Her broken heart needed
mending, and "Mr. Fix-It" Brandon was sure he was the man for the
job....

#1080 ALMOST TO THE ALTAR—Neesa Hart
Elise Christopher and Wil Larson had almost made it to the altar years
ago. Now, fate had unexpectedly reunited them, giving them a chance
to recapture their romance. But would they make it down the aisle
this time?

FAST CASH 4031 DRAW RULES
NO PURCHASE OR OBLIGATION NECESSARY

Fifty prizes of $50 each will be awarded in random drawings to be conducted no later than 3/28/97 from amongst all eligible responses to this prize offer received as of 2/14/97. To enter, follow directions, affix 1st-class postage and mail OR write Fast Cash 4031 on a 3" x 5" card along with your name and address and mail that card to: Harlequin's Fast Cash 4031 Draw, P.O. Box 1395, Buffalo, NY 14240-1395 OR P.O. Box 618, Fort Erie, Ontario L2A 5X3. (Limit: one entry per outer envelope; all entries must be sent via 1st-class mail.) Limit: one prize per household. Odds of winning are determined by the number of eligible responses received. Offer is open only to residents of the U.S. (except Puerto Rico) and Canada and is void wherever prohibited by law. All applicable laws and regulations apply. Any litigation within the province of Quebec respecting the conduct and awarding of a prize in this sweepstakes maybe submitted to the Régie des alcools, des courses et des jeux. In order for a Canadian resident to win a prize, that person will be required to correctly answer a time-limited arithmetical skill-testing question to be administered by mail. Names of winners available after 4/28/97 by sending a self-addressed, stamped envelope to: Fast Cash 4031 Draw Winners, P.O. Box 4200, Blair, NE 68009-4200.

OFFICIAL RULES
MILLION DOLLAR SWEEPSTAKES
NO PURCHASE NECESSARY TO ENTER

1. To enter, follow the directions published. Method of entry may vary. For eligibility, entries must be received no later than March 31, 1998. No liability is assumed for printing errors, lost, late, non-delivered or misdirected entries.
   To determine winners, the sweepstakes numbers assigned to submitted entries will be compared against a list of randomly pre-selected prize winning numbers. In the event all prizes are not claimed via the return of prize winning numbers, random drawings will be held from among all other entries received to award unclaimed prizes.

2. Prize winners will be determined no later than June 30, 1998. Selection of winning numbers and random drawings are under the supervision of D. L. Blair, Inc., an independent judging organization whose decisions are final. Limit: one prize to a family or organization. No substitution will be made for any prize, except as offered. Taxes and duties on all prizes are the sole responsibility of winners. Winners will be notified by mail. Odds of winning are determined by the number of eligible entries distributed and received.

3. Sweepstakes open to residents of the U.S. (except Puerto Rico), Canada and Europe who are 18 years of age or older, except employees and immediate family members of Torstar Corp., D. L. Blair, Inc., their affiliates, subsidiaries, and all other agencies, entities, and persons connected with the use, marketing or conduct of this sweepstakes. All applicable laws and regulations apply. Sweepstakes offer void wherever prohibited by law. Any litigation within the province of Quebec respecting the conduct and awarding of a prize in this sweepstakes must be submitted to the Régie des alcools, des courses et des jeux. In order to win a prize, residents of Canada will be required to correctly answer a time-limited arithmetical skill-testing question to be administered by mail.

4. Winners of major prizes (Grand through Fourth) will be obligated to sign and return an Affidavit of Eligibility and Release of Liability within 30 days of notification. In the event of non-compliance within this time period or if a prize is returned as undeliverable, D. L. Blair, Inc. may at its sole discretion award that prize to an alternate winner. By acceptance of their prize, winners consent to use of their names, photographs or other likeness for purposes of advertising, trade and promotion on behalf of Torstar Corp., its affiliates and subsidiaries, without further compensation unless prohibited by law. Torstar Corp. and D. L. Blair, Inc., their affiliates and subsidiaries are not responsible for errors in printing of sweepstakes and prizewinning numbers. In the event a duplication of a prizewinning number occurs, a random drawing will be held from among all entries received with that prizewinning number to award that prize.

SWP-S12ZD1

5. This sweepstakes is presented by Torstar Corp., its subsidiaries and affiliates in conjunction with book, merchandise and/or product offerings. The number of prizes to be awarded and their value are as follows: Grand Prize — $1,000,000 (payable at $33,333.33 a year for 30 years); First Prize — $50,000; Second Prize — $10,000; Third Prize — $5,000; 3 Fourth Prizes — $1,000 each; 10 Fifth Prizes — $250 each; 1,000 Sixth Prizes — $10 each. Values of all prizes are in U.S. currency. Prizes in each level will be presented in different creative executions, including various currencies, vehicles, merchandise and travel. Any presentation of a prize level in a currency other than U.S. currency represents an approximate equivalent to the U.S. currency prize for that level, at that time. Prize winners will have the opportunity of selecting any prize offered for that level; however, the actual non U.S. currency equivalent prize, if offered and selected, shall be awarded at the exchange rate existing at 3:00 P.M. New York time on March 31, 1998. A travel prize option, if offered and selected by winner, must be completed within 12 months of selection and is subject to: traveling companion(s) completing and returning a Release of Liability prior to travel; and hotel and flight accommodations availability. For a current list of all prize options offered within prize levels, send a self-addressed, stamped envelope (WA residents need not affix postage) to: MILLION DOLLAR SWEEPSTAKES Prize Options, P.O. Box 4456, Blair, NE 68009-4456, USA.

6. For a list of prize winners (available after July 31, 1998) send a separate, stamped, self-addressed envelope to: MILLION DOLLAR SWEEPSTAKES Winners, P.O. Box 4459, Blair, NE 68009-4459, USA.

EXTRA BONUS PRIZE DRAWING
NO PURCHASE OR OBLIGATION NECESSARY TO ENTER

7. The Extra Bonus Prize will be awarded in a random drawing to be conducted no later than 5/30/98 from among all entries received. To qualify, entries must be received by 3/31/98 and comply with published directions. Prize ($50,000) is valued in U.S. currency. Prize will be presented in different creative expressions, including various currencies, vehicles, merchandise and travel. Any presentation in a currency other than U.S. currency represents an approximate equivalent to the U.S. currency value at that time. Prize winner will have the opportunity of selecting any prize offered in any presentation of the Extra Bonus Prize Drawing; however, the actual non U.S. currency equivalent prize, if offered and selected by winner, shall be awarded at the exchange rate existing at 3:00 P.M. New York time on March 31, 1998. For a current list of prize options offered, send a self-addressed, stamped envelope (WA residents need not affix postage) to: Extra Bonus Prize Options, P.O. Box 4462, Blair, NE 68009-4462, USA. All eligibility requirements and restrictions of the MILLION DOLLAR SWEEPSTAKES apply. Odds of winning are dependent upon number of eligible entries received. No substitution for prize except as offered. For the name of winner (available after 7/31/98), send a self-addressed, stamped envelope to: Extra Bonus Prize Winner, P.O. Box 4463 Blair, NE 68009-4463, USA.

SWP-S12ZD2

As seen on TV!
Free Gift Offer

With a Free Gift proof-of-purchase from any Silhouette® book,
you can receive a beautiful cubic zirconia pendant.

This gorgeous marquise-shaped stone is a genuine cubic
zirconia—accented by an 18" gold tone necklace.

(Approximate retail value $19.95)

Send for yours today...
compliments of ❤ *Silhouette*®
™

To receive your free gift, a cubic zirconia pendant, send us one original proof-of-
purchase, photocopies not accepted, from the back of any Silhouette Romance™,
Silhouette Desire®, Silhouette Special Edition®, Silhouette Intimate Moments®
or Silhouette Yours Truly™ title available in August, September, October, November and
December at your favorite retail outlet, together with the Free Gift Certificate, plus a
check or money order for $1.65 U.S./$2.15 CAN. (do not send cash) to cover postage and
handling, payable to Silhouette Free Gift Offer. We will send you the specified gift. Allow
6 to 8 weeks for delivery. Offer good until December 31, 1996 or while quantities last.
Offer valid in the U.S. and Canada only.

Free Gift Certificate

Name: _____

Address: _____

City: _____ State/Province: _____ Zip/Postal Code: _____

Mail this certificate, one proof-of-purchase and a check or money order for postage
and handling to: SILHOUETTE FREE GIFT OFFER 1996. In the U.S.: 3010 Walden
Avenue, P.O. Box 9077, Buffalo NY 14269-9077. In Canada: P.O. Box 613, Fort Erie,
Ontario L2Z 5X3.

FREE GIFT OFFER   084-KMD
ONE PROOF-OF-PURCHASE
To collect your fabulous FREE GIFT, a cubic zirconia pendant, you must include this
original proof-of-purchase for each gift with the properly completed Free Gift Certificate.

084-KMD-R

WELCOME TO SILVER CREEK COUNTY

A place full of small-town Texas charm, where
everybody knows your name and falling
in love is all in a day's work!

Award-winning author **SHARON DE VITA** has
spun several delightful stories full of matchmaking
kids, lonely lawmen, single parents and humorous
townsfolk! Watch for the first two books,
THE LONE RANGER
(Special Edition #1078, 1/97)
and
THE LADY AND THE SHERIFF
(Special Edition #1103, 5/97).
And there are many more heartwarming
tales to come!

So come on down to Silver Creek and make
a few friends—you'll be glad you did!

Look us up on-line at: http://www.romance.net   SE-SILV1

The collection of the year!
NEW YORK TIMES BESTSELLING AUTHORS

Linda Lael Miller
Wild About Harry

Janet Dailey
Sweet Promise

Elizabeth Lowell
Reckless Love

Penny Jordan
Love's Choices

and featuring
Nora Roberts
The Calhoun Women

This special trade-size edition features four of the wildly popular titles in the Calhoun miniseries together in one volume—a true collector's item!

Pick up these great authors and a chance to win a weekend for two in New York City at the Marriott Marquis Hotel on Broadway! We'll pay for your flight, your hotel—even a Broadway show!

Available in December at your favorite retail outlet.

NEW YORK
Marriott®
MARQUIS

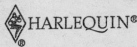 HARLEQUIN®  *Silhouette*®

NYT1296-R

returns with

HONEYMOON HOTLINE
by
Christine Rimmer
(Special Edition #1063, 11/96)

NEVADA JONES WAS AN EXPERT ON LOVE...

...in her professional life. But in her personal life, she's
stayed away from the dangerous emotion—except for
one unforgettable night in the arms of Chase McQuaid.
She's been running from him ever since, but Chase is
determined to catch her—and teach the "love expert"
a few lessons she'll never forget....

Don't miss **THAT SPECIAL WOMAN!** every other
month from some of your favorite authors and
Silhouette Special Edition. Coming soon...

A LAWMAN FOR KELLY   **ASHLEY'S REBEL**
(Special Edition #1075, 01/97) (Special Edition #1087, 03/97)
by   by
Myrna Temte   **Sherryl Woods**

You're About to Become a

Privileged Woman

Reap the rewards of fabulous free gifts and benefits with proofs-of-purchase from Silhouette and Harlequin books

Pages & Privileges™

It's our way of thanking you for buying our books at your favorite retail stores.

PROOF OF PURCHASE

SSE-PP20

Offer expires March 31, 1997

Harlequin and Silhouette—
the most privileged readers in the world!

For more information about Harlequin and Silhouette's PAGES & PRIVILEGES program call the Pages & Privileges Benefits Desk: 1-503-794-2499

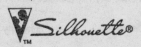

SSE-PP20